W9-CSG-721

SOCCER TOMMIES

BASEBALL MOMMIES

G. Mitchell Baker
With Jane Carroll

 Master Koda Select Publishing

Soccer Tommies, Baseball Mommies

An MKSP Book/July 2014

Published by Master Koda Select Publishing, LLC
www.masterkodaselectpublishing.com

Originally published in eBook form by Master Koda Select Publishing in 2014

ISBN-10: 0990587800
ISBN-13: 978-0-9905878-0-4

Cover design © Jacqueline Cross, Master Koda Select Publishing
Cover images © Tornado: npclark2k / http://www.morguefile.com
Soccer ball: wintersixfour / http://www.morguefile.com
Baseball: alexispuentes / http://www.morguefile.com

Acknowledgement/Appreciation

I played a lot of baseball when I was a kid, soccer in college. My appreciation begins with the Baseball Mommies and Soccer Tommies who attended the many games. I played on championship teams that produced National Hockey League stars (Lindy Ruff, David Babich), one Olympian (Terrence Danyluck, volleyball) and we played against the likes of Wayne Babich (NHL hockey), and Tim Chen (World Champion Baseball). Tim pitched against me and helped me become a decent hitter. In my estimation, there were at least three other ball players who could have played Major League Baseball. It remains my honor to have competed with such talented athletes who inspire through their proven competitive drive and sportsmanship.

As for this book, the inspiration also came on a sunny Saturday in San Diego. Tim (pitcher for Taiwanese National Baseball and design engineer for the World Champion Nissan GTP Racing), Jeff (front Office of the San Diego Padres), and I broke away to play some pick-up baseball. Oh, and there was Kinny (my Border Collie - 1996-2012) who played hard, chased and shagged baseballs usually hit out into the middle of nowhere. She played with all her heart, and showed us about playing The Game with a full spirit. My remembrance remains fond.

On that San Diego Saturday, Tim, Jeff, and I went to our usual park and arrived as a little league baseball team squared off with a girls' soccer team. They haggled over whose field it was to practice on that morning. The title *Soccer Tommies, Baseball Mommies* immediately came to mind. I wrote the story as a feature length screenplay and completed it just before my daughter was born. This story is for Gaelen, Garrett, and all the friends they may make given the potential to share this work among friends.

All these years later, I must thank Jane Carroll, Author of *Bertha Size Your Life!* and *On Becoming Bertha* (Master Koda Select Publishing, 2014) for helping me adapt this young adult story from screenplay to middle-grade novel. Jane helped me deal with a lot given I was a mere mortal writing about baseball, soccer, and tornadoes in the same book. I also thank Kim Mutch-Emerson, Author *Digitus 233* (Master Koda Select Publishing, 2013). Jane and Kim's tough love made it possible for me to write a decent story.

As for this story, I wrote it to encourage kids to play hard and be decent to others, despite all the frustrations and distractions that happen along the way. Through this fun loving tale about kids and towns overcoming tragedy and peculiarity, I hope kids learn there is always more to 'winning' than simply posting 'W's' in the 'Win Column'. I am thankful for all who have put up with me through the years, and hope this story brings fond memories. May you, who I have come to appreciate, always be, 'Where you are supposed to be … doing what you are supposed to be doing … when you are supposed to be doing it...'

A special thanks to the Master Koda Select Publishing Team, including Kim, Rebbekah, Arlene, DeEtte, Jackie, Tamy, Jazz, and all the rest of you good-natured rabble-rousers of the written word.

Chapter 1

The Down the Mountain Wheelie

The next morning everything was a goin' and a blowin' in all the wrong directions, but that did not stop Tape. Teddy watched as Tape pulled back into a wheelie and zoomed from the Adam's Mountain Highway, his blond hair flowing from underneath his helmet. He mysteriously turned into Teddy's driveway, gently put down the front wheel and slowed. Teddy jumped down from the deck and grabbed for his bike. Tape hollered with a grin, "You Reddy-Reddy Teddy-Teddy?"

Teddy swung his bike around and waved. "Let's hit it!"

The roar and cheer of a stadium crowd from inside Teddy's home interrupted any takeoff when Tape paused. Sounding puzzled he asked, "Hey, what was that?"

"SST," said Teddy.

"What's that?"

"Some serious *Soccer Trauma*," Teddy explained.

"Serious what," asked Tape.

"Terri's watching one of her stupid DVDs. She might be my twin sister, and the other half of the *Fab 2,* but her thing with soccer is more than any baseball-playing brother should have to endure."

"She's really into that stuff?" Tape dropped his bike in disgust.

"*Obsesso Traumatico,*" said Teddy as his ball bag hit the ground.

"Talk English man," Tape badgered. "*Obsesso whatico?*"

"C'mon," Teddy waved. "I'll show you."

The noise grew louder as they climbed the steps and crept across the red wood deck. Crouched behind the woodpile, Teddy and Tape had a view of the living room big screen as they listened. "…and the right forward …oh my, look at the great speed from the right outside. What confidence. What ball control."

"What is that?" Tape whispered.

"The 1999 Women's World Cup Soccer Match between the United States and China. I figure it was the beginning of the end of the world as we know it."

Tape considered the possibilities. "It's a soccer game from before we were even born?"

"Yes sir."

"What's the big deal?"

Teddy guessed his best friend thought she looked cute or something in her oversized World Cup Soccer jersey with the letter "C" on it. They both watched her practice her soccer footwork to the final moments of the World Cup Match. Her red, white, and blue soccer ball bounced and balanced as they listened to the stadium crowd cheer madly.

"And the USA forwards push up on the attack...."

Tape stared at Terri. His eyes bugged out as his mouth dropped open.

"Hey Tape," Teddy muttered, "You interested in the soccer or my sister?"

"It's all good," Tape looked away sheepishly.

"Who or what exactly is 'all good'?" asked Teddy. Tape knew Teddy would not let him off easy.

"Look!" Tape gasped. "She's taking off her shirt?"

"Who is?" Teddy's head snapped.

"She is." Tape pointed. "Look!"

"I don't think so," Teddy balled his fists, ready to defend the honor of his sister as Tape ogled the USA soccer player, who just scored the game winning goal. She had been running in celebration and then slid on her knees while she pulled her jersey over her head.

"She took off her jersey and threw it in the air!" Tape stammered, "She's like … like a soccer machine!"

"What the--" Teddy swallowed hard, "There are soccer machines?"

Tape ignored the question. His eyes were back on Terri as she tapped the soccer ball from her right foot to her left foot. The ball arched gracefully through the air on each pass. It was all so romantically automatic. "Kind of like a comfortable machine or something," Tape pined.

Still thinking he might need to defend Terri anyway, Teddy stood. The movement startled Terri and Teddy's Border Collie Kinny. The dog caught sight of the boys out the corner of her eye. Terri executed a back flick with the soccer ball and smirked as the ball arced over her head and came to rest on her right thigh.

"Whoa! You see that?" gasped Tape. "That is the ultimate soccer cool pose!"

Teddy rolled his eyes, and looked away as Terri maintained her cool pose and then tossed a wave to invite everyone to join her in the family room.

"No way," snapped Teddy.

"Why not?"

"This is the very threat to the fabric of civilization as we know it," said Teddy. "Hel-lo. This *Soccer Tommie* is t-r-o-u-b-l-e?"

"But she is good," whined Tape.

"Forget this. Let's get to practice."

"Do we have to go?"

"We have to go now." Teddy led the way back to the bikes. "You have to be strong. You have to resist the lure of the *Soccer Tommies*, whenever and wherever they appear."

Chapter 2

The Skunksters Invade

Teddy grabbed up his bike and slung his bat bag over his shoulder. The sun was bright and strong as Tape asked, "Why is it girls play soccer and guys only baseball in Belleville?"

"Duh man," Teddy scoffed. "Girls decided they wanted to be good at soccer and we decided we wanted to stay good at baseball."

"So the Dominion Daughters wanted to do their own winning."

"Sure." Teddy did not finish his thought as he saw a mama skunk and four skunksters bounce across the lawn. They headed for the deck steps. "Look out!" Teddy jumped back.

Tape stopped cold and nodded.

From a safe distance, Teddy and Tape watched as the mama and babies waddled and hopped up the deck stairs. Then they crossed the deck with a sniff and snort as they paraded along.

Teddy and Tape crept backwards, away from the deck. Then they watched as the skunks entered the house through Kinny's doggie door. Teddy pushed his glasses back in place. "Tape, what we have here, is the serious potential for *Odiferous Trauma*."

"We have to get Terri outta' there." Tape rushed toward the deck, scampered up the stairs, and headed for the glass deck doors as Teddy tackled him. "Why?" Teddy pinned Tape to the deck. Then Teddy flashed a mischievous grin that dared Tape to rescue the Soccer Tommie.

"Even your own sister? Unbelievable."

Teddy held "the look" on him and then got up. He then held up the hand signal for a Special Forces creep advance as he led Tape toward the glass deck doors.

"Where did they go?" Tape peered over Teddy's shoulder.

Terri dribbled her soccer ball unaware of what was going on.

"Don't know." Teddy strained to look into the family room, past Terri, and into the kitchen. Just then, the skunk family, with tails held high, marched past Kinny's full bowl.

"It's not the food," said Teddy. The black-and-white invaders made a full-on advance into the family room. "Oh, this could get so very interesting."

The boys pulled back from the glass doors leaving finger and nose prints all-over. "What are the Skunksters doing?" Tape sputtered.

"Complaining about all that soccer nonsense," Teddy scoffed.

"But Terri won't hear them over the TV," gulped Tape. "We gotta' do something like go in and save her." Tape drew in a deep breath.

"Hello. Hello!" Teddy grabbed Tape's arm.

"'Hello' what?" said Tape. "We gotta' do something! We can hold our breath and--"

"Tape," Teddy's voice lowered. "We are not the Navy SEALs. Besides, holding your breath is not going to help any."

"Why not? I'm ready, Teddy."

"Besides," said Teddy, "SEAL Team 6 would not go on a mission that involved skunks."

"You think Team 6 would refuse a mission?" Tape balked.

Unaware of the danger at hand, Terri showed off her best soccer moves as the last of the baby skunks made the turn and disappeared into the family room. Tape and Teddy went back to the window. Then Kinny dropped her Frisbee and short-stepped toward the skunks.

"You are about to witness the single most devastating event in Fabiano Family history." Teddy patted his belly, often referred to as the "Bobo." The sense of satisfaction was huge.

"And Kinny," demanded Tape. "What kind of pet guy are you?"

"Oh yeah," Teddy thought for a moment. "Kinny...."

"You gotta' care about her man," Tape pleaded. "I mean even if you gotta' be a Pirate who doesn't care about your soccer sister and all."

"Alas, poor Kinny," Teddy's head lowered. "Unfortunately, that's what she gets for hanging around the Soccer Tommies instead of going to baseball practice with us."

Engrossed in her soccer practice, Terri noticed Kinny had abandoned her Frisbee. Then Terri saw what had Kinny's attention, and she let out a great scream.

"Here we go!" Teddy enjoyed the drama as Terri faked a boot of her soccer ball at the Mama skunk. Instead of scaring the skunk, Terri looked on in horror as the skunk instinctively turned and locked her tail in place, prepared to defend against the threat of the soccer ball.

Kinny yipped as the first skunk perfume hit her nose.

Terri watched as the four baby skunks followed Mama's example and one by one flipped around and snapped their tiny tails into place. Terri freaked as the line of locked and loaded skunksters wiggled in the direction of her and Kinny. It was now the epic Soccer Tommies versus the Skunksters showdown.

"The very nerve," Terri kicked the soccer ball with all her might and blasted Mama Skunk square in the butt. Fortunately, the ball arrived fast enough to catch most of the noxious skunk's spray.

Teddy announced into a pretend microphone, "And oh my! What a classic shot-on-skunk by the young lass from the USA. Unfortunately it was not enough to settle the attack of all the Skunksters."

The smelly ball rolled back towards Terri and Kinny; the thought of retreat was automatic.

"Did you know a skunk's spray is flammable?" Teddy pretended to interview Tape.

"Really?"

"Yes sir with lots to ignite around here too."

Tape nodded. "Wait! What if this all catches on fire and--?"

"Enough already." Teddy's nod was calm. "Nothing is going to explode."

"Okay then." Tape settled as Teddy continued in his best announcer voice. "Soccer Tommies 1 and the Skunksters Nil."

"Look," Tape exclaimed as Terri's second soccer ball blast knocked the squealing Mama skunk butt-over-tea-kettle and clear back into the kitchen. Surprisingly, the babies stood their ground and remained ready to fire again. With head down, and tail between her legs, Kinny started toward the front line of determined baby skunks.

"Kinny. No!" Teddy shouted, as Terri grabbed Kinny's fluorescent green Frisbee with one hand and Kinny with the other. With the disc held in front of them like a shield, Terri attempted to jump out of the way just as the four baby skunks let go with their tiny shakes and smelly sprays. The close range showers of putrid perfume hit the Frisbee and caught Kinny's tail flush.

Teddy slumped to the deck in laughter as Kinny yowled and tried to crawl under the coffee table.

"What you laughing at?" Tape demanded.

"Didn't you see those baby skunksters?" Teddy bawled. "There were those little twitches, and then Booosh Ka-Pow, *el Stinko Rama-Jama!*"

"But you have to live in this house," Tape reminded him. "Everything you own is going to smell like skunk!"

"Oh man." Teddy jumped up and flew into action, but Tape pushed him aside, no longer the reluctant hero.

"Tape wait," Teddy cautioned. "What are you doing?"

"I'm going in!"

Startled by Tape's rescue attempt, Terri clutched Kinny's collar and dragged the dog through the flustered skunksters and toward the opening deck door. She knocked Tape flat on his butt on her way out. He scrambled, and then sat up, face to face with the Mama Skunk. "Ahhh ... wait for me!"

Outside, Kinny jumped from Terri's arms and ran for a patch of green grass. When she got there, she rolled and whimpered to get rid of the skunk stink. Terri followed, dropped to her knees, and slid along the grass. She looked exactly like her hero, Brandy Chastain on the World Cup DVD.

"Terri, you alright?" Tape ran to her side. "Hey. Wait! You gotta' leave your shirt on!"

"Why a freakin' skunk?" Terri bawled. "With all the wildlife on this stupid mountain, why not a possum or a squirrel?"

"You alright or what," Teddy demanded coolly.

"I'm calling the paramedics," yelled Tape.

"Is this a 9-1-1 situation?"

"Okay smart guys," spouted Tape. "You got another plan to get a bunch of fired up skunks outta' your house?"

Wide-eyed, the Fab 2 looked at each other, and then turned to Tape and the Skunksters. At the same time everyone yelled, "Call 9-1-1!"

Chapter 3

Old Luke Comes to Call

It was the next morning and Kinny got hungry and decided she would come home stinky or not. Then Teddy had to scrub her down with tomato juice. He scrubbed as he held his breath. Had to breathe again and endure the stink, then scrubbed Kinny some more.

"Dang," Teddy fussed. Unfortunately, he had yet to realize that the skunksters were not going to be the only tough-time the Fabiano's would experience. He took some time to figure out there was a right way and a wrong way to soak and wash Kinny. Close to finishing, he thought he could clean up his mess. Suddenly, the Belleville Tornado warning siren filled the chilled air with a drawn out wail. The mechanical voice sounded. "Tornado … take shelter now. Tornado … take shelter now!"

Teddy grabbed up Kinny, her tomato-juiced fur felt slimy. Everyone scrambled for the Fabiano Family storm shelter. Buried deep in the mountain rock of the front yard, Teddy knew there would be safety if they reached it soon enough.

He glanced around and saw Mama and Papa Fabiano hurry toward the shelter. Then Terri came into sight. Teddy did not want to, but finally looked over his shoulder and saw the giant funnel shape disappear into what was now a dirty darkness in the middle of the day. The tornado would soon be on top of them.

As the Fabiano family arrived at the cellar door, the wind pushed everyone around. Teddy held Kinny tight as she struggled to get loose. She wanted to run as far away as possible.

Then Teddy noticed how the air did not feel right. His ears wanted to pop. It got deadly calm. Nothing looked like it was moving. The storm was near … so near it was still.

Suddenly the storm began to breathe. The sounds of the wind through the trees grew louder and then there was an instant roar. "Climb down," Papa Fabiano yelled. "Get in. We have to close the door!"

Teddy and Kinny stepped down and in as the storm cellar door slammed shut. Teddy heard the bolt slam and lock into place. Finally secure, Teddy could not help but think something very bad was going to happen.

At once, a hot, moist air stirred and mixed with the churned cool air of the cellar. A no-doubter of a huge storm was coming on, and bearing down fast!

Holding a squirming Kinny tight, Teddy waited for someone to say something. The only sound to fill the cellar was the deafening roar of the extreme storm. Then Teddy remembered from his school report how the Japanese called the wind he heard the "Devine Wind" or "Kamikaze." As far as he was concerned, the Kamikaze winds could just leave them alone. After what seemed like forever, Papa Fabiano yelled, "Everyone doing okay?"

Not knowing why he said it, or even to have an idea where the thought came from, Teddy yelled back, "A half hour in this storm cellar can age a kid forty-nine years!" Only then was he aware that the dog he still held on to tightly, not only smelled of skunk, but also reeked of tomato juice. Teddy looked around the cellar and was comforted to know he was not the only one about to puke his ever-loving guts out all over the storm cellar floor.

"Don't you dare puke," yelled Terri. She stared Teddy down.

Teddy knew that to add the stench of vomit to the skunk and juice odors would surely be the end of the Fabiano Family. "Don't you worry," yelled Teddy, "Pirates don't puke. It'd be a waste of good rum!"

"Okay now," Mama Fabiano spoke up to change the subject. Just then, Papa received a strong signal over the weather radio. "Listen up!"

The radio announcer described tornado touchdown after touchdown as the storm, now nicknamed "Old Luke," seemed to last longer than most. Teddy reached a breaking point. "I can't stand the smell!"

"Settle down Teddy," commanded Papa Fabiano.

"I'd rather take my chances with Old Luke than stay in here another second!"

Kinny squirmed from Teddy's loosened grasp when he reached for the cellar door.

"Just sit yourself down." Papa pointed to the chair. "If you would have stopped those skunks from going in the house, we would not have to deal with the smell. Now suck it up and hunker down!"

Teddy sat in his chair, relieved that Papa had called his bluff. Old Luke did not sound like a force he wanted to reckon with, even with the skunk and tomato smells and wind noise and all. "Sorry Papa," Teddy said in earnest. "I had no idea it would get this bad."

Terri pinched her nostrils together while trying to cover her ears from the wind wail. "Kinny's smell is nothing compared to my soccer ball! It's your fault!"

"Kids," Mama Fabiano bellowed, "the storm, the smell, the mess upstairs is all bad enough without you bickering. Settle down!"

"Yes ma'am," the Fab 2 replied in unison, only to shoot each other nasty looks. After what seemed like an eternity of potential puking, the radio announcer proclaimed it safe to leave the skunkified shelter. The warning siren and the obnoxious mechanical voice suddenly stopped.

One by one, the Fabiano family stepped up and out into their changed world. The air could not have been fresher, as the cool breeze washed over the back of Teddy's sweaty neck. He looked over to see Papa, who also breathed in deep as he surveyed the downed trees, the debris cast off by the tornado's hyper-spinning action. Mama Fabiano just repeated, "Our home is okay. I am so thankful our home is okay."

Teddy looked for Terri. She had already made her way through the broken trees and fencing and stood at the mountain edge of the property. There, she looked down on the town of Belleville.

Teddy made his way over branches and part of someone's doghouse. Soon, the Fab 2 stood together and gazed upon the town. "I think that was G-McMa's doghouse for Purdue," Teddy offered, sadly.

"Jeeze Teddy," Terri choked, "what's left?"

The twins only listened enough to hear the radio in Papa Fabiano's hand. The reports continued. "Belleville was not so lucky. Early reports estimate damage to the Town of Champions to be in the millions of dollars. It appeared that Old Luke had zigged, paused, and zagged its way around the town. And there are reports of injuries, and perhaps--"

"Who ever heard of a tornado doing a slow dance through a town our size?" fumed Papa Fabiano.

They all looked on, and decided to go down into the town and learn more about the actual damage. "Wanna' ride down the mountain to check things out?" Teddy was already looking for his helmet and bike.

"Sure," said Terri.

"Be very careful." Papa provided permission, through the warning given, "stay out of the way of emergency vehicles and workers."

"Let's check out the fields," said Terri. "I may not have a ball, but I still want to go to practice tomorrow." Terri shot Teddy a look that reminded him everything until now, including the tornado and smelly storm cellar was his fault.

"You think there will be practice?" Teddy asked.

"There always has to be practice. We always have to practice."

The Fab 2 found their helmets and bikes and then rode down Adam's Mountain. They had to be careful as they dodged downed branches and all kinds of broken things called 'Tornado Debris' by most. When they rounded a curve, they hit the brakes in time to avoid an overturned boat.

"Whoa! That thing is huge!" Teddy jumped off his bike, and just stared at the massive boat belly.

"Think we should go back?" Terri placed her right foot down and leaned into her bike for balance.

"Well we can't go through the boat," reasoned Teddy. "I think we are going to have to wait a day-or-two--"

"Until this tornado-junk is cleared away," interrupted Terri. "Let's go back and help Mama and Papa clean up at the house."

"Guess I gotta' finish up with Kinny, huh."

Terri looked over, as if suddenly reminded of the sorry Skunksters chapter in the Fabiano Legacy. "Of course you have to."

Teddy nodded. For some strange reason he thought that because of Old Luke, someone was going to volunteer to do his chores. Terri did not say anything. Teddy was sure she was thinking about it, given they had both been through a tough time with skunks and juice and tornados and boat bellies and all.

"Of course you have to," Terri repeated. "What do you think this is … anyhow?"

Chapter 4

The Change in Everyone's Lives

The third day after Old Luke had performed its wicked dance of damage through Belleville, the Fab 2 set out again to check out the demolition. Terri and Teddy pedaled down Adam's Mountain and right onto Main Street Belleville. "Over there," Terri pointed to the roofless hardware store covered with blue tarp that lifted and rolled in the stiff breeze.

"Can't be good," Teddy pedaled faster. Then he got a stitch in his gut. "My Bobo is cramping tight."

"Oh no," exclaimed Terri. "Look!"

With a quick glance, they saw some folks picking up belongings dropped when they scrambled for safety. Others looked for things that were still lost after being carried everywhere by the storm.

Teddy and Terri rode past the Belleville Sports Store and it looked okay. Nate Abelard was outside and swept away the dirt and debris piled up against the building. Then the Fab 2 saw the boarded windows on the nearby Murray's Coffee Shop. They could hear a generator from around back. "Look," Teddy pointed as Mayor Sydney Tabbshey came out of the newspaper office next door and readied himself to hand out bottled water and bags of ice. "Kids, you need any water … ice?"

"No thank you Mr. Mayor," said Terri.

Across the way, Caleb's Tire Store was broken apart something fierce. Scattered for miles around, new and used tires were located and gathered to be stacked into round black towers. The Fab 2 rode along and saw perfect houses and businesses next to piles of rubble. Then there were the places that were not there anymore. It looked like they had never existed.

"How can this be?" asked Terri.

"It's this way all over town," replied the mayor.

"What *Definite Destruction Trauma*," Teddy said quietly. "What--"

"That will be enough," Mayor Tabbshey suggested. "Here. Have this water."

Teddy received the water and handed it to Terri. "Here. Have some water."

Terri reached for the water as church bells rang loud to signal the clean-up workers to finish their lunches. Before long, there were chainsaws again revving and blaring everywhere. A four-wheeler driven by Caleb pulled a trailer full of cut branches in a race along Main Street. Terri and Teddy stayed out of the way, only to dodge a broken swing-set and then ride over part of a sign from Rudy's Game Shop. They rode the full length of Main Street. They slowed, as they got closer to their planned destination. Had the soccer fields survived? What about the Old "B?"

Before long, they learned the answers. There, they saw Grandma McIvor, the eighty-seven year-old town mother who sat by herself, rocking on her cluttered porch. The kids waved, but there was no wave in return. The twins sensed something was not right. They stopped and then heard her crying with grief. "G-McMa," Teddy hollered. "What is the matter?"

"Where's Purdue?" Terri yelled as she bolted through the fence gate and on to the porch. Teddy immediately began to gather up broken branches and debris. Terri looked for a broom. Teddy saw a white square patch in the grass left, after Old Luke took up Purdue's doghouse.

"Where is Purdue?" Terri asked again.

G-McMa lowered her head in despair. Teddy had never seen such sadness. They all knew if Purdue was gone for three days, the chances Old Luke got him were good. Then Teddy recalled the part of the doghouse that he had helped clear from the Fabiano yard. He figured it had to be Purdue's house. He then thought how sad Kinny was when they loaded the broken wood pieces into the truck. "This is not good," Teddy murmured.

"We'll help you find him." Terri hugged G-McMa, and then looked over to her brother. They knew it was time to search, while they checked the playing fields. "We have to go."

The Fab 2 said nothing as they rode along. Terri stopped in front of a dangling sign that read, "Dominions Daughters" through the scraped off and mud-covered letters. "Oh my," Terri started to cry as Teddy pulled up beside his sister. With a huff and puff given the quick ride from G-McMa's house, he announced, "It can't be all that bad."

"The sign," Terri stopped sniffling, as eerie silence settled around them. Each looked up to see the piles of Old Luke's

Tornado-Junk growing into mountains.

"Oh man." Teddy looked on. "The soccer fields are gone and buried." It looked like something from a dark, science fiction story.

"Oh yeah," Terri looked on, with tears in her cool, blue eyes. "Look at all that tornado-junk."

"Awe, don't cry." Teddy did not know what else to say, so he snapped at her like a big brother. "For a Soccer Tommie you can be such a girl sometimes."

Terri did not say anything. In a way, Teddy was glad she did not look up as he struggled to hold back his own tears. He would not let Terri see him as a weak big brother.

"I bet they can fix it up in no time," Terri tried to convince herself, but then could not take it anymore. "Come on. Let's go look for Purdue and see about the Old 'B'."

"Let's go." Teddy led the way. His thoughts filled with scenes of the damage and the people Old Luke had hurt. There was the ruined kid's playground and then they saw the cell phone tower had toppled over. The twisted wreckage caught part of the water plant as it fell.

"So that is why our cell phones aren't working," said Terri.

"Look," Teddy pointed. "It just missed the water tower."

Moments later, the Fab 2 approached the Main Street Gate to the Old 'B' and found it open. The Fab 2 hopped off their bikes and saw the green grass, pitcher's mound, home plate, and the scoreboard. "Old Luke spared the Old 'B'," Teddy crowed. "Get a load of that beautiful field."

"It's not fair," cried Terri. "You stupid Baseball Mommies get all the breaks!"

"Of course it's fair," Teddy argued. "The Dominion Daughters could not stand up to Old Luke the way us Pirates did. Baseball is superior to soccer and it is simple as that!"

"No it's not," maintained Terri. "I'm going to see Mayor Tabbshey. We'll see what he says!" Terri spun around, grabbed up her bike, and took off.

"Wait," Teddy hollered. "We have to check in on G-McMa and keep looking for Purdue."

Terri rode off, not wanting to listen to anything her brother had to say.

"Now why did she have to go and do that?" Teddy mumbled under his breath. "Old Mayor Tabbshey is just gonna' say a lot of something about nothing anyway."

It was not long, before the Fab 2 saw Mayor Tabbshey still outside Murray's Coffee Shop. He held out a bottle of water. "Here, take it."

"No thanks," said Terri as she stopped and dropped her bike. "Just need to know how soon the soccer fields will be cleared and fixed-up again."

Teddy straddled his bike and listened as the mayor indicated his appreciation for the concern. Then he said something about how he and the Town Council had to set priorities for repairs based on priority. Terri frowned when the mayor told her, "What's most important to the town as a whole, is that we have strong priorities."

She argued. "Then I guess the soccer complex will be fixed right away."

The mayor stumbled, "Um. Well … it may be a priority, but--"

Teddy wanted to encourage a meaningful response. "Just tell us when the soccer fields will be fixed-up, mayor."

"Well, that's just it," Mayor Tabbshey stammered.

Nate Abelard, the owner of the Belleville Sports Store walked up to listen for a moment. Then he spoke. "I think what the mayor is trying to tell you, is that there are other things that have to be fixed before we can work on the soccer fields. As you know, our town was blown up by Old Luke and we have had to deal with dead animals, injured people, businesses torn up, and utility problems. The mayor here is handing out water, because we are worried about contaminated water. I understand that the town loves sports. No one loves this town's sports championship legacy more than I do. However, our biggest worry is not the soccer fields. Perhaps we can call a town meeting to talk about the fields, but it will be some time before we can get to it as a priority."

Teddy looked over to see Terri again tear up. It was all just too much for her to handle. Shoot. Teddy was not so sure it was all becoming more than he could handle.

"You know kids," suggested the mayor, "what you need to do is go check on G-McMa. I heard she can't find Purdue." Mayor Tabbshey stroked his handlebar mustache and curled the ends tight.

"We were there," said Teddy. "Been looking and we're headed that way again."

"Purdue is gone," Terri took in a deep breath. "We will help her find him."

"Good … right," said the mayor. "And thanks Nate."

Nate nodded. "Kids, we have to work on some things around town. Then we will get to the fields. Okay?"

"That's right," Teddy agreed.

However, Terri scowled. "What could affect the town more than soccer?" Her face was as red as the fire hydrant next to her. "We have a big tournament coming up, and it brings in thousands of dollars--"

"We do realize the importance of the Dominion Daughters," said Nate, "and of soccer in general. There are just so many things damaged that--"

"Even City Hall has roof damage," said the mayor, as he pointed to the orange tarp stretched to cover part of the building.

"But there are so many of us. So many teams," complained Terri. "We have games scheduled, and we are ranked to be state champions again. What can be more important than competing for--?"

"Unfortunately, it is not a priority," answered Mayor Tabbshey. "City Hall is the most important building in our town. I'm sorry." The mayor lowered his head as Teddy jumped in. "So what'll they do, forfeit all their games?"

"Not at all," Nate answered. "Mayor Tabbshey and the town attorney will work out a plan so the Dominion Daughters can continue their season."

Terri's eyes brightened. "Okay when? Let's have it."

"Well, Mr. Litton and I," said the mayor, "will create a visitation plan, a joint custody agreement for the Old 'B'."

"This is not a divorce," Teddy interrupted.

"Son, I know it isn't, but it won't be long before there will be a lot of people who want the same thing and they cannot all have the same things. Therefore, they will have to share. I know they will not want to share, but the Pirates and the Dominion Daughters will have to share the Old Belleville Ballpark equally."

"Share the Old 'B'," Teddy exclaimed.

"We'll call it the *Field Visitation Agreement*."

"No way," Teddy and Terri shouted.

"That didn't take long." The mayor shook his head. "I'm afraid you won't have a choice, unless either side wants to forfeit their season." Nate placed a hand on each youngster's shoulder. "It's really the only fair thing to do."

The Fab 2 nodded in unison, neither able to speak. Teddy swallowed hard. "It's not the only thing, Mr. Nate. It's not the only thing we can do at all."

"Not by a long shot," Terri sounded determined.

"Now do not forget about Grandma McIvor and Purdue," reminded the mayor.

"We're on our way," Terri assured, with a nod in Teddy's direction. "We'll go make sure she's okay and then head back up Adam's Mountain.

Chapter 5

Best for the Town

The next day the Fab 2 dropped in to Murray's Café for a soda. The boards were gone from the windows, and the sun shone in as the kids reported to the mayor that they did not find Purdue. They also had to tell Mayor Tabbshey that G-McMa was still very, very sad.

With the news, the mayor turned to Nate and was quickly distracted with something going on outside. "So what is best for the town right now?"

Teddy and Terri listened carefully, as Tabbshey answered his own question. "I'm thinking what is best for this town, is to keep everyone safe and to continue the clean-up."

"I agree with you mayor," said Nate. "This just is not going to be easy. That's all I'm saying."

Some of the town elders sat comfortably and rested a little more before they left the coffee shop. "Hey mayor, what you gonna do about the soccer field? What's left of it, that is?" Rupert asked as he passed their table.

"Who is that," the mayor asked Nate.

"That is Andie's uncle," Nate whispered.

"Oh okay," the mayor was satisfied, and then continued with his answer. "The soccer fields will continue to be used as a collection point for all the tornado-junk. In the meantime, lawyer Litton and I have worked up a visitation schedule so the Dominion Daughters and Belleville Pirates will share the Old 'B'." Tabbshey tweaked his mustache, and then looked up and down the diner counter for a response to poll.

"You've got to be kidding," Bertha hollered from across the café. "The Belleville Pirates have a championship to defend. They cannot share the field with tomboy soccer players. They need to practice and play their games. Have you thought about that?"

"We have," Mayor Tabbshey addressed the room. "Lawyer Litton will speak with the division offices for soccer and baseball to see whether they will agree to work with us to accommodate both teams."

Teddy looked over at Terri, and she seemed quiet, perhaps disheartened.

"The Dom Dots also have a championship to defend," Rupert argued. "I swear. You Baseball Mommies make me so mad. All you think about is yourselves."

"Yeah, well go defend your championship on your own turf and leave the Old 'B' alone. It has been all about baseball for longer than most of us can remember. In fact, the 'B' is one of the original steel and concrete stadiums in the country and built for b-a-s-e-b-a-l-l. Not freaking soccer!" Bertha pushed her plate away.

"Calm down." Nate sat straight. "Old Luke was an accident, an act of God. None of us knew it was coming, or could prepare for it. Everyone knows that tornadoes skip around demolishing one building and leaving the one next door unharmed. It could have just as easily been the other way around--"

"Like what?" Bertha challenged.

"Well how about trying to figure out how to fix the soccer field instead of sharing the ball park?"

"That's right," the mayor chimed in, grateful for Nate's help. "The tornado took a lot away from everyone. What I see are many folks on edge. We just have to figure out the best way to get right back to ordinary Belleville living. I for one am going to get right back out there and see what I can do about getting those utilities right and clearing more roadways."

"Can I quote you on that, mayor?" Cary, the local newspaper reporter, asked from the corner. The mayor put on his biggest campaign smile. "Cary, that won't be necessary. I will be monitoring things and working out the kinks as they show up."

"Well, here's a 'kink' for you," Bertha piped up, still not happy with the situation. "How's practice gonna work? Our boys practice from sunup to sundown during the summer. It is all they want to do. Eat and practice baseball. How are they gonna get their practice?"

"They won't." Nate took the question. "But neither will the girls. Both teams will have to give, in order to take. They have to learn to share the field."

"That sounds an awful lot like my divorce decree," Rupert quipped. "I can tell you it don't work all that well."

Heads around the café nodded in agreement, so Mayor Tabbshey changed the conversation. "Joe, Old Luke got your house, didn't it?"

"Yes sir. A huge tree branch landed right in the middle of the living room. We sure were lucky we were in our shelter." Joe lowered and shook his head. "Old Luke squashed the place like it was a bug or something."

"Y'all able to live there … I mean in your wrecked house?"

"Not even close. We have talked to the insurance man and they will pay, but it's gonna' take time to get the check. And then with so much damage everywhere, we will have to wait for a contractor."

"So where y'all staying?" asked the mayor. The conversation was going just as intended.

Joe smiled, with a nod to the man at the next table. "Mack and his family have made room."

"It's crowded, but we're glad to help our friends and neighbors," said Mack. "It could have just as easily been my family and Old Luke and that tree."

"Isn't this the same thing?" Nate sat his coffee cup on the counter. "Isn't this what the mayor is asking us to do … help friends and neighbors?"

Rupert and Bertha stood to argue and Rupert started. "No … it's not the same thing at all."

Then Bertha argued, "Dang Soccer Tommies!"

"Blasted Baseball Mommies," was the shout from somewhere in the diner. "It won't work!"

"Stupidest thing I ever heard."

"Coach LaFleur will have something to say about this all right."

"She has something to say about everything," said Rupert.

"They can't make us."

"Coach Shimpock won't stand for it--"

"We'll see…."

"Glad I didn't vote for you, Tabbshey," rumbled Rupert.

"Sure won't next time," said Bertha.

Teddy and Terri sat listening. It took a while before the loudest people left Murray's Cafe. Teddy looked on as Nate and Tabbshey hunkered down at a table to the rear of the restaurant. He listened, as Nate said to the mayor, "I'd say that went about as well as expected." Nate patted Mayor Tabbshey on the back as they got up and walked out of the coffee shop.

"Those Soccer Tommies and Baseball Mommies sure know how to pick a side and argue it."

"Not like anything we haven't seen before, mayor," Nate reassured.

"Not like anything-- What about that time Old Mr. Wallace brought that pet possum down off the mountain and right in here during breakfast that Sunday morning?"

"Well that certainly caused a stir."

"It sure did. And now we have a Possum Ordinance that says, 'No Possums shall be allowed in any eating establishment in the Town of Belleville'."

"I do believe we are the only town in America with a 'Possum Ordinance'."

"You are darn tooting," grinned Tabbshey "The only town indeed."

Chapter 6

Practice, Anything But Usual

Late that afternoon, Teddy looked up from behind his catcher's mask. He saw Coach Marcie LaFleur crouch in a kind of hitter stance over home plate. She squeezed the bat with her long red fingernails that pointed straight. Her fingers did not curl around the bat handle.

Nobby, a new kid from India seemed fascinated or something as Teddy threw him the ball. The new kid could not take his eyes off the weird fingernails. Teddy listened as Nobby clucked, "Coach, you are pretty versatile." Teddy guessed he meant she had adapted to being a coach with long fingernails. After all, it was a wonder she could hit the ball at all. She always amazed the Pirate baseball team when she connected with a hit.

"Good catch, Nobby!" Coach LaFleur shouted, as Nobby threw the ball to Teddy behind the plate. "Great play, guys. We are champions today!"

The practice went on, as Coach LaFleur hit the ball and the team executed play after snappy play. However, once confident they would beat the Cougars in their season opener, Tape started to throw fat pitches that made for easy hitting practice. The Pirates were definitely distracted.

It was then that Coach LaFleur broke her number-one rule. She took her eye off the ball and broke a nail with a loopy, empty swing. The fuss to follow was enough for the Pirate practice to appear done for the day.

The Pirates stood around and watched Coach LaFleur do the broken nail dance at home plate. It was not a pretty thing to observe, let alone for Teddy to be within ten feet of as he stood and waited behind the plate. He wondered what was going to happen next as Coach Shimpock, along with a couple of the Soccer Tommies, began to half-drag and half carry a large soccer goal toward the Old 'B' outfield. They positioned the goal to the right-field side of the scoreboard and headed back for the second goal.

"Wait just a minute!" Coach LaFleur forgot about her nail and sprinted to the outfield. Teddy watched as she rolled her fingers and her good fingernails clicked intensely.

"What do you think you are doing?"

Coach Shimpock stopped and turned. "We're setting up for practice according to the Field Visitation Agreement. I was hoping for an efficient transition of theater operations."

"No you are not," battled Coach LaFleur. "We still have thirty minutes on the field. The agreement doesn't say anything about you setting up early." One by one, the Pirates abandoned their positions to stand behind Coach LaFleur.

"Coach, please. We agreed not to leave the goals in place between practices, but it takes time to get them set up," replied the Marine drill sergeant. "We have to start a few minutes early, or the kids won't be able to get in a full practice before dark."

"And we're supposed to give up practice time to accommodate you?" LaFleur stood on her tiptoes and shouted directly into Shimpock's chiseled face.

"Honestly, you don't have to stop practice. We'll just quietly set things up and you all finish up and--"

"No way," argued LaFleur. "Is it our fault your Soccer Tommies need goals moved around? Being in the outfield disrupts our concentration and makes the boys miss plays. Besides, the Visitation Agreement says--"

"I know what it says. I thought--"

"No. You did not think," lectured LaFleur. "If you had 'thought', you would know you cannot disrupt the Dominion's practice. It is bad enough you are taking over our field. But I'm gonna' tell you it is not gonna happen while we're still on it!" Coach LaFleur spun and stomped across the field as the Belleville Pirates fell in behind.

Teddy looked back to see Coach Shimpock wince and remain silent in front of his players.

The Dominion Daughters gathered and Shimpock continued to lead by example. "Okay, Dom Dots," Teddy could hear as they marched along with LaFleur. "Get the goal off their field."

"Come on boys," Coach LaFleur yelled. "Play ball!"

Having forgotten about her broken nail, Coach LaFleur soon had the Pirates practicing again. Teddy stood, watching the ball thrown from player to player. In the back of his mind, a question nagged

Teddy. *Had the defense of the Belleville Pirate home field advantage been too successful?*

The ball came to him and he tossed it to Coach LaFleur. There were no words spoken between them. It was then Teddy knew the Baseball Mommies were serious about keeping the Soccer Tommies off the Old 'B' as much as possible.

Chapter 7

The "Good" Sports Store

The next day Teddy rode hard and until his bike jumped the curb and skidded sideways. It did not stop until it hit the bench in front of Nate's Sports Store. Embarrassed, Teddy thought how it sure beat a sideswipe from the Fuller's Brake and Auto Supply truck that sped down Adams Mountain Highway, and nearly got him along Main Street.

With all commotion put to rest, Teddy checked for bike damage and complained, "You'd think a brake shop truck would know how to use their brakes."

Nate came out of his store to check on things and overheard Teddy's complaint. "A lot of people are out of control since Old Luke blew through these parts."

"What's a tornado got to do with crazy driving?" snapped Teddy. He shoved his bike in the rack.

"C'mon in," invited Nate as he turned back toward the store's door.

Teddy followed Nate in. "People just don't seem to know what's what anymore."

A Belleville police car whizzed by with flashing lights and siren blaring. "There goes Deputy Measure," said Teddy.

Nate closed the door and watched Teddy head over to "The Counter of Success."

"You really predict athletic success of us kids from behind this counter?" asked Teddy.

"Sure do," Nate beamed. "My dad started it when he opened the store back in 1954. I picked up where he left off. Altogether we have correctly predicted four Major League ball players, two NFL players and an Olympic gold medalist in Track and Field."

"No soccer players, huh?" asked Teddy, mischievous.

"Not yet," Nate hung a soccer jersey on the rack. "But your sister has been predicted to have the holding and promise."

"So you predicted, here at the Counter of Success that Terri will go up the ladder?"

"She's one tough, talented player."

"What about me?"

"You tell me. Are you one tough, talented ballplayer?"

"Oh, yeah," answered Teddy, and then he changed the topic. "Now I remember why I came by. How much for the best soccer ball you got?"

"I 'got'?" Nate arched his eyebrows.

Teddy figured Mr. Nate did not like the poor grammar.

"You have," corrected Teddy.

Nate smiled. "The best ball I have is $37.50. It is the one she had before--"

"You know about--?" asked Teddy curiously.

"Stinky news travels fast. Those Skunksters gave everyone in Murray's something to joke about over coffee. Shoot, we all need to get our minds off of Old Luke some time."

"Everyone but Terri," added Teddy.

"I suppose."

"She's not laughing," Teddy explained. "So I wanted to buy her a new one. All I've got is fourteen bucks and some change."

"Tell you what," said Nate. "You come back when you have got a little more, and we can work something out. After all, we can't have the first Major League Soccer player from Belleville if she hasn't got a ball to practice with."

"We sure can't Mr. Nate," said Teddy, his eyes brightened. "And she won't be able to do any endorsements either."

"Really," Nate scoffed at the notion of the ball used for a commercial.

"I will work something out, and I'll be back before you know it. Can you hold the ball for me?"

"Consider it done." Nate met Teddy eye-to-eye and they shook hands. "Teddy, you're doing the right thing."

"Thanks, Mr. Nate," said Teddy proudly. "You know Terri's all right for a girl, and being a soccer player and all."

"You know son, the right thing isn't about soccer or baseball or boys or girls. It is about doing the right thing regardless of what you like or dislike. Does that make sense?"

"I think it does," Teddy gave an honest answer. "But don't tell anyone about this talk today … okay?"

"Sure. Good. Now you go figure out how to make it all happen." Nate opened the door and Teddy rushed out, grabbed up his bike, and headed up Adam's Mountain with thoughts of raising more money to replace Terri's skunked up ball.

Chapter 8

Two Practices and a Munch

About a week after Old Luke hammered Belleville for about twelve minutes, Teddy walked with Nate along Main Street. They saw families playing in what was left of the children's park.

They arrived at the Old "B," and through the Main Street Gate Nate looked over the ball field before he stepped onto the hallowed ground. Teddy followed and saw Nate take in a deep breath of the cool, damp, ballpark air. "So the Dominion Daughters set up their nets and practice until the Pirates come and take the field?" asked Nate.

"Yes sir," was all Teddy answered as they went silent and listened.

"Dominion, to the line," commanded Coach Shimpock.

A half-hour later Nate offered, "I have to get going. Have a good practice."

Teddy continued to watch the Dominion Daughters finish their practice with waves of wind sprints. Kinny paced the players around the dugout where the Pirates were gathering and starting to toss the ball from one player to the next. The faint stench of old skunk filled the air as Kinny raced past and the Pirates laughed when Spider shouted, "That skunk smell is punishment for playing soccer!"

Teddy went down to the dugout and sat with the others who had said their piece. He then leaned forward to tie his cleats and looked over to Munch, the Pirate mascot. Munch was Chris Verney's Saint Bernard. With a bright blue Belleville Pirates collar, Munch ambled over to the bat pile and plopped down to chew on the handle of his favorite. An old, busted Sam Bat that one of the Pirates had received when they went to watch a Major League game. Teddy sat back against the cool concrete of the dugout wall. He looked around as Munch abandoned his bat and bolted past the ballplayers to join the last wave of Dominion sprinters. "Hey Munch," Teddy hollered. "Make up your mind! You wanna' be a hitta' or you wanna' be a runnin'?"

Out in the field, Kinny snapped at Munch's heels to keep the intruder away from the Dominion players. "All right," Coach Shimpock clapped sharply, "good practice Dominion! Start your cool down and do not forget to get these poles and nets out of the way so the Pirates can take the field."

The Dom Dots collapsed in the cool grass as Munch wandered between the players. Despite Kinny's efforts to herd Munch away, the Saint Bernard watched and waited for a water bottle to drop to the grass. As soon as Terri dropped her bottle, Munch drooled his way over to it and lapped the cool moisture from the side of the bottle. When that was not good enough, Munch bit down hard on the bottle and ice water squirted everywhere.

"Munch, you stupid ol' dog," Terri turned to the Pirates across the field. "Hey you *Nine Inning Ninnies,* when you going to get a real dog for a mascot?"

This is not going to be pretty, thought Teddy.

As Munch stirred things up even more than usual, Teddy looked around for Chris to gather up his dog. Instead, Teddy saw Chris with his dirty blond hair grab up a Frisbee and sprint across the diamond. It looked like Chris tried to show off in front to the girls as he flipped the Frisbee through the air. "Here Terri," Chris hollered.

"Oh great," Teddy frowned.

"What… a trade or something?" asked Terri.

"Naw, toss it," grinned Chris. "Munch will get it."

Andie Sanchez, with hair cropped short, had a smile to dazzle. She hollered, "No way. Munch will tear it apart. That is, if he even gets it."

"Why not?" asked Chris. "Why wouldn't he get it?"

"Too dumb," said Andie.

Chris put on his best defiant cool pose. "Toss it. We'll see."

Munch eyed Terri's weak Frisbee toss, and then lumbered along uninspired. Kinny flashed past Munch in a blur of black and white fur and caught the Frisbee before it hit the ground. Munch's brow dropped as he stopped short, to avoid the lingering skunk odor. Kinny dropped the Frisbee to the grass and Munch advanced slowly to snatch it up with a big "munch." With his head high and proud, Munch galloped back to Chris.

In the background, Teddy could hear the Dominion Daughters only jeer. The louder the girls got, the faster Munch galloped. The faster Munch galloped, the more the Frisbee flipped up to plaster against his face. Munch ran faster and faster as the Dominion Daughters and the Pirates cheered and jeered. It was suddenly obvious Munch could not see where he was going. "Watch out," Chris yelled. The galloping dog headed straight toward a goal post.

Chris ran and dove to tackle Munch, but it was too late to save the chugging canine. Munch ran straight into the goal post. The head-on collision caused a loud, dull ring, like a muffled bell. The onlookers grew quiet as Chris ran up and wrapped his arms around the old dog. "Munch, you okay?"

Munch appeared dazed, and with a soft yowl tried to stand, but staggered backward as if in a stiff breeze. He then looked up into Chris' worried eyes. The Pirates gathered around, concerned.

"Concussion rule is in effect," sneered Georgia. "Means Munch can't chase a Frisbee until he's cleared by a vet."

The Dominions laughed and the Pirates shot back their best swashbuckling sneers. Suddenly, slaver and slobber flew everywhere as Munch shook off the effects of the impact. Relieved, both the Dominion and the Pirates yowled to celebrate the mascot's recovery.

"Hope he doesn't really have a concussion," hooted Chris. "He could have brain damage."

"Doesn't he have to have little gray cells for 'brain damage'?" Georgia grinned.

"That ol' dog is no Frisbee dog," scoffed Terri.

"Yeah, but when he gets 'em he holds on to 'em!"

"When he does get a hold," ridiculed Andie. "Wait … you mean 'a hold' of the Frisbee or of the little brain cells?"

Everyone laughed as Chris kicked the grass with his cleat. "I'll show y'all how ol' Munch here can get them." Then Chris muttered under his breath to Munch, "You're a Frisbee dog all right." Munch happily sauntered along at heel to Chris. The soggy Frisbee dangled limp from his mouth, his prize catch for the day … well anyway … maybe sort of a catch.

The other Pirate ballplayers finished with their equipment as Coach LaFleur arrived with a cell phone plastered to her ear and without pause, she fast-walked past the dugout, through the infield and into center field. There she charged at the exhausted Dominion Daughters.

"Oh this is not going to be good," said Teddy for all to hear.

"Not good at all," Chris agreed, "Things could be worse, but they could also be a whole lot better."

Chapter 9

The Pirate's Push to Practice

Tape and then Nobby hustled to Coach LaFleur. Teddy joined up at the pitcher's mound and listened as Coach grinned. "Nobby, baseball players tuck in their shirts." Teddy rolled his eyes and hoped his coach was not going to get on the new kid's case. Then he looked over to Nobby and smiled as Coach LaFleur finished her thought. "Son, ball players tuck in their shirts … always, but you don't have to tuck in your hoody."

"That's right 'Son'," said Tape, with a Southern drawl. "You don't have to tuck in the hoody."

Part of the team laughed and relaxed, while Teddy and a few others held up as Coach LaFleur marched off to center field to scold the Dominion. "C'mon you Soccer Tommies … get up, and Go! Go! Go!"

"'Soccer Tommies'?" shouted Terri.

"You are not the Dominion coach," bawled Georgia, her box twists whipped furious as she looked around for Coach Shimpock.

"Girls you are delaying America's *National Past Time*," Coach LaFleur continued. "Move it!"

"'America's National Past Time'?" repeated Andie.

"Baseball," Coach LaFleur leered.

"More like *America's National Bed Time*," dared Terri, frustrated as LaFleur's long fingernails clicked and ticked. From where Teddy stood, the *rikki tik tik* of his coach's nails was a sure sign she was ready to argue back. There he saw Coach Shimpock enter into the fray.

"Coach LaFleur, what can we do for you?" Coach Shimpock seemed cautious, perhaps respectful. However, LaFleur ignored him and yelled again, "We need all the daylight we can get girls. Now hustle on home."

"'Hustle on home'?" repeated Coach Shimpock, surprised. "Lady you ever heard of respect?" Shimpock, now the Marine, crowded LaFleur. "Just have your *Baseball Mommies* back off here and let the soccer team warm down so they can all get going in the right direction."

"Why you overblown bag of hot air," railed LaFleur. "Just because you are a Marine, doesn't mean you can throw that big handsome chest around and--"

"Getting kind of personal here, aren't you coach?" Shimpock crossed his arms across his chest. His stare locked onto Coach LaFleur, as both teams braced for a battle of wills.

"Hmmm, well, 'Yes'." Coach LaFleur looked up toward the Center Field Gate and smiled as she saw Mrs. Shimpock march right through the gate and toward her husband, Coach Shimpock. The color of her cheeks matched her red shirt as she bellowed, "Did you forget about the parent-teacher meeting after school?"

Sheepishly, Coach Shimpock nodded in the direction of his wife.

Tape walked over to stand next to Teddy and they made eye contact. Then Teddy whispered to Tape, "This Marine is going to need a lot of 9-1-1." Teddy pressed his glasses up to his nose.

"What you mean?" asked Tape.

Teddy looked serious. "Coach Shimpock is about to experience some serious *Marine Mama Trauma*. That would mean we need to call 9-1-1 and get some First Responders out here on the double."

"Ohhh," Tape nodded. "Huh. Gonna' get bad?"

The boys watched the events unfolding and held their breath.

Mrs. Shimpock made her way across the field and to the pitcher's mound. It was her show now and Coach LaFleur could not resist. "Come on, coach. Are you going to move things along here or not?"

Coach Shimpock sputtered.

"You know, given the Field Visitation Agreement and all."

"But--?" stammered Shimpock.

"It's the efficient transition of theater operations we're looking for here," LaFleur grinned. "So very important you know."

"Mark, you coming?" demanded Mrs. Shimpock.

"The Dominion Daughters will warm down," Shimpock decided.

"Nope," LaFleur argued. "The deal is the Dominion Daughters are out by 16:30 hours and it is 16:35."

Mrs. Shimpock moved to stand beside Coach LaFleur. "It is the law Coach Shimpock and we are supposed to be at our meeting."

"Rather be playing than arguing," said Teddy. All in the background heard what he said and nodded as then talked in low tones.

"And," argued LaFleur, "If we start with an exception here, then who knows where this will all end up."

"Zowie," exclaimed Tape. "Coach Laf is bringing it ... Bam Ka-Pow!"

"And he is toast," Teddy nodded. "Brutal, she is absolutely brooo-tal."

The Pirates remained uneasy. Some smirked nervously and others kicked at the red dirt as the Dominion Daughters looked on in stunned silence.

"This visitation stuff is nuts," Tape proclaimed. "Will I have to testify in court or anything like that?" All the kids laughed, nervously.

"C'mon coach." Mrs. Shimpock led Coach Shimpock toward the Main Street Gate. "Darling, the field now belongs to the Pirates."

Chapter 10

After Soccer Practice

The next day, Terri and Teddy rode to the Belleville Sport Shop. Terri dropped her bike on the sidewalk as Teddy put his in the rack. When they entered the store, Nate looked up and asked, "Is it true?"

"What's 'true'?" asked Teddy.

"The shirt."

"You mean mine?

"No not you," Nate waved Teddy off.

"A *Louisville Slugger* for sure, big time. That's me."

"I meant Terri's shirt."

"Huh?" Terri scrunched her face.

"Does seven days without soccer really make one weak?" asked Nate.

Terri tried to read her shirt upside down. "Oh … I guess it's true, because seven days without a soccer ball has left me weaker by the minute."

"Sorry about your ball." Nate opened a box of Belleville Pirate ball caps.

"You heard about that?" Her shoulders dropped.

"Of course, the story of Terri versus the Skunksters has spread through town faster than Old Luke. It's legend." Nate began to build a display with the caps.

"That stinks," said Teddy.

Terri frowned.

"Well, I guess I'm the cause for some *Serious Odiferous Trauma.*" Nate grinned. Then Teddy grinned as Terri rolled her eyes to the ceiling. "Give me a break."

"So what can I do for you today?" asked Nate. "Here to buy a new ball?" Nate pointed to an array of soccer balls across the store.

"No sir not today. Mama and Papa do not seem to think it is a priority. We don't have much money since Luke caused a lot of stuff to be fixed," Terri said unhappily.

"Well, don't give up. Something may just work out before you know it." With a sly twinkle, Nate changed the subject. "How did practice go today?"

"It was pretty screwed up," said Terri.

"What do you mean?"

"To start with," Teddy explained, "Coach Shimpock and some of the players tried to get there a few minutes early and get the goals in place. We really wanted to start on time."

"And...?"

"And Coach LaFleur wouldn't let them," Teddy continued. "Only this time, Mrs. Shimpock showed up and there was the *Marine Mama Trauma.*"

"Doesn't sound pretty," commented Nate.

"They were goin' on and on about the Field Visitation Agreement." Terri slumped against the Counter of Success.

"Sounds kind of serious," Nate frowned.

"It really was," Teddy agreed.

"I'm not used to seeing grownups argue," Terri shrugged.

"But nobody lost it, did they?" Nate confirmed, as he walked behind the Counter. "A lot of people are stressed right now."

"You got that right," agreed Terri. "You know the worst part?"

Nate shrugged and listened.

"The whole time they were goin' on, nobody got to practice," complained Terri.

"It was just wasted time," confirmed Teddy, as Mayor Tabbshey entered the store.

"Indeed," Mayor Tabbshey mumbled, "I was not impressed."

"Didn't hear you come in, mayor." Nate turned. "Been here long?"

"Long enough," Mayor Tabbshey tweaked his mustache.

"Nice to see you, Mr. Mayor," Terri smiled politely. "Guess I need to be pedaling up the mountain. Thanks for the chat."

"You're always welcome to stop by." Nate waved. "Hang in there. I have a feeling things will work out."

Terri left the store as Teddy settled in to listen, while the mayor and Nate continued their conversation, "Do you believe that?" Mayor Tabbshey asked. The door closed after Terri.

"Yes, I do," Nate nodded. "We've got a way to go to get things right in this town again."

Nate considered the Dominion Daughter's polo shirt and Belleville Pirates cap in a nearby display.

"My friend," the mayor continued, "I'm going to try and be fair and do what's right."

"I wish everyone in Belleville felt the same way," Nate nodded.

"You don't think they do?"

"Not by a long shot. It's time to earn your salary and change some minds around here," joked Nate.

"So it's my job to fix this mess?"

"Sure--"

"Then that is what I will do," said Tabbshey.

"That is why I voted for you," smiled Nate. "If anyone can fix it, you can."

"And what do you think about that, Teddy?" asked the mayor.

"We sure have to fix things around here," Teddy answered.

"Well I agree," Mayor Tabbshey nodded seriously. "It's time to come up with a serious game-plan."

Chapter 11

Slow Down

Teddy swept at the driveway. His heart was not into the project as his mind wandered. After a while, he glanced up to see Deputy Al Measure park his car on side of the road, just down the mountain. The deputy positioned his car just uphill from the Founders' Day banner that marked the end of Main Street and the beginning of Adam's Mountain Highway.

Teddy paused to watch, as the deputy aimed his radar gun at a gray sedan. Deputy Measure shook his head and Teddy figured he was not happy. Most Saturday mornings, Deputy Measure found everyone in a hurry to get nowhere fast. Teddy was sure he was used to issuing a number of citations from that very spot. However, this morning it was vehicle after vehicle that drove by at or below the speed limit. Teddy knew why the cars slowed, but was not going to volunteer to Deputy Measure there was anything peculiar.

Eventually, Deputy Measure opened the door and stepped from his car. Then the familiar Fuller's Brake and Auto Supply truck drove slowly through the mountain switchback. The driver smiled and waved, as he made his way down the mountain without a traffic stop.

Teddy knew well that Eddie usually drove the Fuller truck like a maniac. It was just last week Teddy had been terrorized along Main Street. Teddy looked over to the deputy, who appeared to decide something was just not right.

Like any good deputy, he investigated. Just into the curve, he saw Teddy. The deputy stepped softly on the pavement, to avoid making crunching sounds.

Teddy followed the deputy's gaze further up the mountain, and they both saw the huge sign that faced the downhill traffic. Measure could not read it from his angle, but suspected it had something to do with the well-behaved drivers.

Teddy hoped his sweeping would be a good excuse to hold up under the deputy's scrutiny. With a wave and smile to the oncoming motorists, Teddy noticed how they pointed behind him, rather than wave back. Slowly, he turned to see Deputy Measure with his intimidating six-foot-two presence bearing down on him. The fact that Teddy could not see his eyes behind NASCAR sunglasses did not mean he could not know the deputy was upset.

"Um… Hello, Deputy Measure," Teddy gulped.

"And what does the sign say?" the deputy asked.

"Uh," Teddy stammered. "Well sir, it reads, uh …I think it says '*SLOW DOWN—RADAR*'!"

"Well, Teddy." Measure walked toward and reached for the sign. "I can't ignore this problem here. What are you doing?"

"Sweeping?"

"Sweeping?" repeated the deputy.

"Sweeping helping," Teddy tried again.

"Now it's 'sweeping helping'?" he asked. "How and who are you 'sweeping helping'?"

"Well, maybe you … them," It was hard for Teddy to think straight as Deputy Measure glared down on him. "The drivers really do need to slow down and we were just getting them to do that for you."

"'We'" Deputy Measure caught the slip. "Who else is with you?"

"Tape," said Teddy.

"Marty 'Tape' Measure?" considered the deputy.

"Yes sir."

"Let me guess. You guys are out to make a buck or two?" Deputy Measure crossed his massive arms.

"No way," Teddy wagged his head.

"Okay then," Measure motioned, "let's take a walk."

"It's hot for a walk, don't 'cha think?" Teddy wiped his brow.

"Not as hot as it's gonna get if you don't catch up here."

"That's what I was afraid of," Teddy grumbled as he joined alongside Deputy Measure.

"This far enough?" asked Teddy.

"I suspect Tape may be the reason the cars are braking just around that bend up there," Deputy Measure waved.

"Oh yeah," said Teddy. "It is such a lovely morning for a walk. I almost forgot we were looking for him."

Measure gave Teddy a 'nice try' look, as they rounded the curve to find Terri in a scramble after money tossed from the open windows of motorists. "I thought you said it was Tape on this end of your operation?"

"It was." Teddy could not believe his eyes. "I had no idea."

Terri received Teddy's *"What are you doing here?"* look and ignored Teddy. Instead, she smiled sweetly at Deputy Measure. "Good morning, Deputy Measure. How are you?"

Teddy stood a couple of steps behind the deputy, and ran his finger in front of his throat in an unsuccessful attempt to warn Terri not to schmooze the officer.

"Okay, kids. What is going on here?"

"Teddy is trying to earn enough money to buy me a new soccer ball," Terri blabbed.

"How'd you know that?" demanded Teddy.

"I figured it out."

"Oh really?" said Teddy, doubtful.

"Tape told me," said Terri. "Then I told him I'd take over. I figured if it is for my ball it should be me. Besides, he had to get home and--"

"So that's what this is all about," a smile cracked through the sour look on the deputy's face. "The skunkster ball needs to be replaced and you are trying to--?"

"You know about the skunks too?" Teddy and Terri asked, as only twins can.

"A good lawman makes it his business to know everything that goes on in his town."He lowered his voice and relaxed a bit. "Besides, next to Old Luke, the skunkster thing is the biggest thing to happen in Belleville recently."

"Tape told you didn't he?" questioned Teddy.

"Sure he did."

"So you understand why we did it?" Teddy's question was hopeful. "You aren't mad at us?"

"I didn't say that," corrected Measure. "This is serious. I told him not to do it--"

"That's why he bailed," Teddy scoffed.

"Not only could you have been hit by a passing car, but you interfered with official police business."

"We didn't think about that." Terri's response was sincere.

"That's the problem. You didn't 'think'," Deputy Measure continued. "You two are student athletes. You are supposed to think things through, and--"

"You played pro baseball, didn't you?" Teddy interrupted.

"I played several sports in my time. And 'thinking' is what they all required." Deputy Measure got back to the subject.

"You played more than one sport?" Terri asked.

"I sure did. In fact, many of the better athletes do."

"Did you play soccer?" Terri asked hopefully.

"No. Soccer had not caught on yet."

"And they called them the 'Good Old Days'." Terri shook her head. "How is that possible?"

"I heard you played for the Yankees!" Teddy puffed.

"For a short time, but my sport career isn't what we're here to talk about."

Kinny raced up just in time to bark, as Tape came into view. Teddy cheered as Tape performed his *Down the Mountain Wheelie.* "Go Tape Dude!"

Tape let go of the handlebars and waved with both hands.

Deputy Measure looked over his shoulder, at first surprised, and then concerned. "What is he doing?"

"That's TDMW," Terri replied

"Tape's Down the Mountain Wheelie," Teddy explained.

"Looks dangerous," said the Deputy.

"Naw," Teddy kicked at the gravel. "He always slows down when he sees our road signs."

Chapter 12

The Pirates' Consult and Concern

The next day was sunny and bright as the Pirates headed to the Old 'B' for practice. Teddy looked over at Tape's sleeveless Moscow State University shirt with "GRADUITUS OR ELSUS" across his chest. Chris walked alongside. "Hi guys," said Tape. "You hear about the Dominion Daughter's team meeting last night?"

"Yeah," Chris complained. "They had hot dogs. Our meeting was catered with rice pilaf and for fun we had to play Dodge-Ball with marshmallows Tape smuggled in with him."

"That whole scene with LaFleur and Shimpock is weird," said Teddy, troubled.

"I heard the Dominion team is majorly ticked at us," reported Chris. "Like they're Zombies or something and want to take over the whole town and--"

"Okay, hold on," Tape interrupted. "So how are we going to deal with *Soccer Tommy Zombies* now?"

"And still compete at the Pirate's highest levels?" Teddy's concern was more about the Pirate's performance than any Dominion intimidation.

The boys, joined by Nobby and Spider, looked to see Munch nearby. They all bunched up at the Main Street Gate at the Old 'B' and peered into the ballpark.

"Look." Teddy watched the Dominion Daughters execute their perfect drills.

From the field, Kinny looked up to see the boys gawk. She stopped her chase of a scuttled soccer ball and barked a sharp warning from the second base area. No one on the Dominion Team broke concentration from the intense drills, so Kinny gathered up the loose ball and bumped it along with her nose. The Pirate teammates looked on as Terri executed a roundhouse kick she learned in karate. The soccer ball shot toward the net like it was on a rope.

"Dang ... Where did she learn that?" asked Tape.

"My Papa," Teddy answered. "We take Karate."

"You take karate?"

"Yeah sure I do."

"Wow," whispered Pete 'Spider' Muller, a timid boy with a ball cap low on his ears. "This I did not know."

"Look," Tape said in hushed tones, "they're like *Soccer Tommie Zombie Machines.*"

"Soccer Tommie Zombies," Chris repeated as Munch rubbed against his leg.

"Don't freak out," Tape directed.

"Oh, freak-out - all right already," Teddy barked, the argument decided.

The Pirates watched the girls charge into precision plays that developed fast, with more aggression than usual. Jaws dropped, as one of the girls tackled Terri to the grass turf. The hard fall caught everyone's attention. Terri stayed down.

Coach Shimpock called out and all could hear, "42 you slacking?"

Andie ran to Shimpock and was at attention before Coach Shimpock, "Aye sir!"

"No tackle is good when you can stay on your feet and accomplish the same task. This is more about *finesse* 42, not wrecking things up!"

"Aye sir."

"Conditioning allows the Dominion to attack with aggressive finesse and to win!"

Suddenly Shimpock ordered, "25 knuckle-ups for that tackle, 42!"

"Aye, sir!" cracked Andie as she dropped to hit the turf and pump perfect knuckle push-ups.

Terri pulled herself up and Coach Shimpock turned his attention to her, "Fabiano!"

"Aye, sir," Terri said. "I'm 110% sir!"

"How did 42 mark-up and tackle you like that? Hit it for a fast lap!"

"Aye aye," Terri jogged off with Kinny to set the pace.

The Pirate players could hardly breathe. Teddy summed up their experience when he said, "Absolutely, undeniably, crunchily, broootal."

"Savage comes to mind," suggested Spider.

"Will they hurt us bad?" Nobby whimpered.

"I think Nobby has something to worry about here," Chris offered.

"Why me?" asked Nobby, he cringed.

"You bet." Chris shook his head. "They'll look for the new guy first."

"Oh leave Nobby alone," scolded Teddy. "I'm going home to get my stuff."

"Yeah," Tape pooh-poohed, "you get to protect yourself with catcher's equipment--"

"Ah, knock it off." Teddy did not look back.

"Coward," mumbled Tape.

Teddy flashed a furious look at Tape, "What's that supposed to mean?"

Suddenly Munch bolted from Chris' side.

"Look," exclaimed Chris, "he's chasing something black with white on it!"

"Oh no," Teddy grimaced. "Not another skunk."

"A skunk," Nobby was wide-eyed, "a pretty fast one, too."

"There such a thing as a speedy skunk?" asked Spider.

"Munch," hollered Chris. "I don't want to have to juice you!"

Chris and the others gave chase.

"Let's save Munch," Spider hollered. He ran to join Tape, Chris, and Munch.

"Count me out," Teddy turned to head home. "I've had enough skunk practice this week."

Teddy could not keep his back turned for long, and watched as the black critter quickly rounded the base of one large oak and scrambled behind another. Munch galloped through the tree stand and bounced off a smaller oak tree. The dog regained its balance and charged after the furry black creature. The Pirates chased and chased, until Teddy heard Chris holler, "You sure that is a skunk? Sure don't move like a skunk."

"Sure doesn't smell like a skunk," reasoned Nobby. However, the question and answer came far too late as the boys hurled and stumbled through the trees. Eventually Teddy saw very little of the furry black creature. Then Munch disappeared.

"Where'd Munch go?" Chris called out.

Then Chris disappeared.

"Chris is gone," Nobby shrieked, as he ran through a patch of scrub oak.

Teddy started toward the place where everyone seemed to disappear.

"We have to find them," Tape charged in the direction Munch and Chris were last seen.

Then Teddy saw Tape disappear and ran up as fast as he could.

"Ahhhhh!" was all Teddy could hear. A moment later, he saw how Tape had fallen off a ledge, about ten feet into a green, swampy slew called "The Chicken-Foot." Tape had narrowly missed Munch, but knocked Chris over as Nobby could not stop and slipped, and then slid over the ledge and knocked Tape down further into the bog and slew.

Spider eventually rose from the gluey mud and saw all were covered head to toe with thick green slime. Dazed and bewildered, some looked up as Teddy appeared at the drop off point, "Well y'all look like some Zombies not having so much fun."

"Oh man," Tape wailed as Munch woofed and started shaking slime and slobber everywhere.

"Gentlemen," said Teddy, "it looks to me like those Soccer Tommies have knocked you off your game."

Just then, a black squirrel appeared up a tree behind Teddy.

"Well look at that," Chris pointed. Munch let go with a huge "woof" and tried again to chase. However, the nimble squirrel knew Munch was not going to get anywhere and just chattered and nattered.

Teddy spoke again from the ledge. "It would appear you were chasing a squirrel."

Tape pleaded. "Teddy you gotta' help us ... can you talk to your sister? Maybe we can--"

"Sure, I talk to her all the time," said Teddy, "just not about on-the-field stuff. And I am certainly not going to talk to her about stuff like this."

"But you have to," Tape whimpered. "You have got to tell them we are nice guys and we--"

Teddy snapped his head around. "Zombie Dude you kidding me?"

"I don't want to be damaged," whined Nobby, as he picked green and brown slewey stuff from around his neck.

"Hey you guys," said Teddy. "Ever since this Field Visitation Agreement it has been *nada communicado* about the field stuff, okay?"

"We are in big trouble," concluded Tape, trying to stand, but he slipped back into the sludge with a "splash."

"Trouble," scoffed Teddy. "You ain't dreamed enough in your lifetime to begin to know the kind of trouble the Dominion will bring down on us before this is all *said and done*."

"I don't want to be smashed," whined Nobby. There was a green glob in his ear he tried to fish out. "Maybe I'll go find a quiet Cricket team to play on, and--"

"Nobby," lectured Spider, "there is no Cricket around these parts."

"Well maybe Croquet," Nobby sniveled, and spit something swampy brown.

"It moved," gulped Spider. "He spit and it … it's swimming away!"

"What in the name of Captain Hook's good hand are you talking about now?" demanded Teddy.

"Let it go boys." Tape's tone was deliberate. "I've seen Terri take on the skunks. She can kick in ways … at places one can only imagine. Just let it go. It may already be too late for us to reclaim our ship."

Teddy's expression went dark. He was ticked-off and had heard enough. He turned back to the slew zombies with fire in his eyes. "So, you are just going to sit, and slide around in that muck? You are going to stay in there and be intimidated by swimming things and the Dominion?"

"Well I--"

"What's the matter with y'all," Teddy demanded. "Now let's get some fire-in-the-gut and get our Pirate stuff together and play some baseball! You know we need to play baseball where we are supposed to play, when we are supposed to play!"

"You make it sound so simple." Tape waded toward the edge of the slew.

"That is because it is 'so simple'." Teddy waved his hands high in the air. "Gentlemen, just get your heads right, get out of The Chicken-Foot, and let's play some baseball! Shoot … just play some baseball, and maybe we'll have a little fun too."

Chapter 13

Red Mud Rumble

When the Dominion practice was over, the soccer players tilted and pushed the goal frames toward the bullpen areas. The Pirate players, some still slimy Zombies showed up, while others who lived close enough, cleaned up and arrived at the dugout. Kinny was relieved there were others who smelled worse.

Some of the soccer players cast the *Stink Eye* at the rag-tag Pirates. Few of the ballplayers dared look the Dominion way, unless there was a good reason. Some Dominion Daughters did not care and relaxed in the grass.

All was fine, and then Coach LaFleur's mini-van hastily drove up and parked behind home plate. She climbed out with her cell phone to her ear. From across the diamond, Teddy heard a Dominion player, "We have got to take that Baseball Mommy out."

LaFleur unloaded gear, and lumbered onto the ball diamond with a bag of bats. She called out, "Get those bases will you?" No one could tell whom Coach LaFleur directed.

"Yeah," snarled Georgia. "So we can warm down in peace."

"Even practice extra," added Terri.

"The uniform girls," Coach Shimpock reminded the girls about respect, even as Coach LaFleur marched through the infield and stood on second base glaring out to center field with hands on hips. She did not say a word, but everyone could hear her fingernails click, click, rickety tick.

"So are we going to sit here and listen to how the *Nine Inning Ninnies* have to own the field right this very minute?" demanded Andie. The comment was overheard and Coach LaFleur crossed her arms defiantly. Then she hollered, "Coach Shimpock!"

Coach Shimpock walked out to second base and said nothing. He did not act interested, so Coach LaFleur turned to home plate. "Teddy, start the practice!"

"Coach--" Teddy paused to question.

"Do it now," yelled Coach LaFleur. The Pirate players ran in and out of the dugout to collect equipment and then hustled to take their positions. Now in and among the relaxed Dominion Daughters, the Pirates quickly performed warm-up drills with grounders cracked off

Tape's bat. The infield was soon alive with chatter and pick-up followed by a toss in one direction or another.

"Coach LaFleur," Shimpock was shocked given how far LaFleur took her disrespect.

"Work on the one-hopper from the plate," yelled LaFleur. She then turned back to Shimpock. "In front of the kids again, coach?"

Coach Shimpock stomped toward the Main Street Gate, as Terri watched carefully. Shimpock suddenly turned to his players. "Dominion you take your time and warm down properly."

"You bet, coach," said Andie.

Coach Shimpock marched alone, toward the Main Street Gate as the Pirates crowded the Dominion Daughters. Tape stood with a batting helmet on, his warm-up a few lazy swings. "We're getting closer," he commented, "What if we hit 'em or something?"

Rather than reply, Coach LaFleur turned to the outfield and zeroed in on Coach Shimpock. "Are your girls leaving soon?"

"When they are ready," said Coach Shimpock. "When ready, they will make the field available."

"I see," LaFleur turned back to the infield and directed. "Spider you take center."

"But coach," cautioned Spider, "a ball can hit someone."

"You take your position," ordered LaFleur. "Stand right in the middle of that gaggle of Soccer Tommies."

"Yes coach," Spider obeyed and jogged into center field, where he stood nervously in the middle of the Dom Dot's icy glares.

Still with green slew flecks throughout his white and brown coat, Munch ambled over to a pile of bats and grabbed up his favorite, Sam. With a crushing bite, he made his way behind home plate and dropped to munch away.

"Tape take your cuts!" hollered Coach LaFleur.

Tape shooed Munch back and moved up to the plate. He bit down on his gum hard as he looked down and over at Teddy. Then he looked up to the pitcher's mound, where Chris waited to throw his batting practice pitch.

"Alright Chris," bantered Teddy, "throw one of those famous marshmallows you call a fastball."

With a kick at the pitcher's mound, Chris prepared to deliver the baseball past the batter. "Here comes the Mushy Mallow!"

In a split-second, the ball reached the strike zone. Tape swung and missed. "Ugh," Tape frowned. He wanted to hit the ball, and hit it hard.

"Kind'a gives y'all that mushy mallow feeling doesn't it," Teddy grinned as he threw the ball back to Chris.

For the next pitch, Tape relaxed and hit a long fly ball into center field. Soon, baseballs skipped and danced like popcorn in and around the Dominion Daughters. Then Tape connected with all his might and hit a towering fly to center field. Pausing, Chris looked back at Tape and then Teddy. Then they all watched as the ball started to drop. "That ball's going to be trouble when it comes down," said Chris.

The baseball fell slowly, then faster and faster from the sky. "We got a problem landing zone," commented Teddy with head back and hands on hips.

Deep in center field, Andie watched the ball fall toward her. She stood and reached to catch the speeding ball. As it arrived, she could not hold on with soft hands. "Ugh!" Andie grunted in pain. The ball dropped at her feet.

Teddy hollered, "Stitch Burn!"

Andie looked at her hands to see the red stitch marks left from the impact of the speeding fly ball. As she looked at the ball at her feet, Kinny barked frantically. The anxious dog scrambled to round-up the evil ball that glowed white in the bright green outfield grass.

Tape and Teddy joined Chris at the pitcher's mound. "Is she nuts?" asked Tape.

"Who, Coach?"

"I mean Andie," Tape said. "Trying to catch the ball without a glove?"

"Oh no," Teddy raised his mask and pointed in the Dom Dot's direction, "They just have a lotta' guts."

"Look," yelled Tape.

The Dominion team all got up and gathered. "That's it!" Terri shouted like a fiery warrior. "Dominion Daughters are you with me!"

Georgia let out a long call, "Dominnnnion!"

The Dominion daughters all had venom in their eyes. They joined Terri to rush the Pirate pitching mound. "Get 'em Dominion," cried Andie, her fist pumped high in the air. The Dom Dots advanced like a well-organized army who would dare to defend the Old 'B' ball field. The Pirate players formed a circle of defense around the pitcher's mound to defend against the attack.

"Look at the Baseball Mommies," Terri jeered. "They are circling their little red wagon."

Braced and hunkered, the Pirates tried to work up their courage, but there was not much to work with as Nobby yelped, "The Soccer Tommies are coming. I don't want to be damaged!"

"We can take 'em," Chris mumbled. Then Andie tackled Teddy and they crashed to the red earth, catcher equipment and all. The ball diamond then erupted in whoops and fits with flailing arms and legs everywhere. The Dominion took it to any Pirate within reach. "This is the end you *Nine Inning Ninnies*," shouted Terri.

Unexpectedly the turf sprinklers began to hiss, but no one heard them given the raucous rumble. Then the hissing got louder as the sprinklers popped up everywhere and sputtered to life. Soon, streams of water chattered free of the nozzles as Andie shrieked, "Nine Inning Ninnies you are done!"

The rumble in the red mud grew in ferocity and intensity. Now the Dominion and the sprinklers attacked the trembling Pirates. The slippery red mud was an equalizer of sorts and it was not long before the players yelled, hugged, clutched, and pushed one another to keep their balance as they tried to get up and out of the red mud.

The mascots had their fun too. Kinny barked and chased Munch around the circle of boys and girls that sprawled and slithered around in the red muck. Both dogs appeared to have a great time with barks and snaps, not at one another, but at the spurts of water from the sprinkler heads.

"Hey, Chris," Terri taunted. "Where's your *Baseball Mommy* now?"

Chris could not do much about the melee around him. Then he saw Coach Shimpock had returned through the Main Street Gate. The worried coach made his way to LaFleur's side. "What are you doing?" demanded Shimpock. "Why are you letting this go on?"

"Uh," muttered LaFleur. Then, as if with an idea, she pulled out her phone. "I'll call 9-1-1."

"Dominion," yelled Shimpock with a sharp clap. There was no response, other than the sounds of a good-natured giggle and rumble.

Coach LaFleur spoke into her phone. "Yes, this is Coach LaFleur. The Dominion Gang just attacked the poor Pirates baseball team." LaFleur listened. "Yes, I said 'The Dominion Gang'." Coach LaFleur listened into her phone.

Coach Shimpock just listened, and then frowned.

"Why yes, the soccer team," said LaFleur, and then she shrieked when a clump of soggy grass flew past her head, "Yes this is at the Old 'B.' Hurry, it is crazy around here!"

Shimpock took a step backward to dodge more mud balls and grass clumps.

"Boys," LaFleur looked up. "Get out of that mud now!"

Nothing changed. The Red Mud Rumble continued with no dog, no boy, nor any girl listening to any coach. All left to ask was, "What are we going to do?"

"Well, I for one," said Coach LaFleur "will wait for the police to arrive. That nice dispatch lady said she'd send over the 'entire Police Force on duty' to deal with any gangs and hooligans here at the Old 'B'."

Chapter 14

The Entire Police Force

Deputy Measure arrived outside the Old 'B'. He parked his police car and he climbed out to stand tall. He heard enough to determine it was indeed a rumble and grinned as he hitched his belt, shook his head, and stepped through the Main Street Gate to see the boys and girls entangled in an all-out, waterlogged red mud rumble. He looked on to see Teddy on a break from the rumble. The catcher, still in his equipment sat off to the side to watch and listen.

All Teddy wanted to do was observe, as Deputy Measure took a heavy step forward. Measure did not appear pleased as his boot sank through the grass and into the red mud under the grass. The deputy looked up from his muddy boot, and then ignored the water from the sprinklers. He marched through center field, toward the pitcher's mound. He looked on as the coaches stood helpless.

As Measure joined the do-nothing coaches, he shook his head given his first hand observation of the water spray, barking dogs, and the kids who giggled and laughed as they flung mud balls and grass clumps everywhere. "Coach Shimpock," Deputy Measure greeted. "Coach LaFleur. Are we having a nice day?"

Before either coach could answer, a yelp came from within the rumble and Terri popped up from the center, covered from head to foot in bloodshot mud. She shrieked and ran across the field, "Sorry … sorry about that."

The coaches and Deputy Measure looked on, along with Teddy. "Did I hear an apology?" asked Deputy Measure.

"Perhaps," replied Shimpock.

"Sounds to be a civil and polite rumble," observed Deputy Measure.

"So," LaFleur turned, "what brings you to this part of town?"

"Oh," the Deputy hitched his belt. "You know the usual boring patrol rounds. And of course there was the 911 call of 'gang violence' to Mrs. Leavy over at dispatch." Measure paused, thoughtfully. "I guess Mrs. Leavy received the complaint, oh about seven minutes ago. I am wondering if I am going to find any 'gang violence'."

"Perhaps you mean the 'hooligans'," sputtered LaFleur. "I'm sure Mrs. Leavy was talking about her dear hooligans. You know she's always going on about hooligan this and hooligan that."

Shouts and giggles erupted from the field as the adults looked over to see the players chase about home plate with the mascots hot on their heels.

"Looks like the kids are blowing off a little steam." Measure raised his head and looked around through his water-splashed glasses.

"A bit perhaps," Coach Shimpock offered.

"Maybe some," said Coach LaFleur.

"Can I count on you to sort this out?" asked Deputy Measure.

"Sure," said Shimpock.

"Coach LaFleur?"

"Why yes," LaFleur volunteered. "You can--"

The kids rumbled, laughed louder as LaFleur repeated, "Oh, yes, you can count on us to sort this out."

"Good," Measure said. "Then maybe we won't have the mayor have to sort the rest of this out."

"You know," Coach Shimpock, volunteered. "I was thinking--"

"Do you really think we need to involve the mayor?" asked LaFleur.

"Perhaps," Measure answered. "If he really needs to be involved, it is because y'all can't keep your chickens in the coop." Deputy Measure nodded, as he completed his conversation with the adults. He then turned his full attention to the kids who started to collapse from happy exhaustion. A watery giggle echoed through the ballpark, as Measure emphasized his decision. "Yep, this blowing off a little steam has me thinking the whole town could use a little more of this." With his sunglasses removed, Measure wiped his glasses as he mumbled. "Yep ... maybe a town meeting to discuss how there is nothing like a little good-natured commotion to help re-set things that are not working so well."

Chapter 15

The Mayor's Turn

Word spread through the town about the Old 'B' Red Mud Rumble. From anything Teddy heard, most in town felt all things were goin' and a growin' in the wrong direction.

The next evening, as sure as Deputy Measure called it, Main Street Belleville was lit and lively with cars and trucks parked close to Town Hall. Teddy watched as folks hurried up the stairs only to disappear behind the large, wooden doors. Once in City Hall, Teddy saw some arrive late and join all who crammed into a noisy meeting room.

After a few more minutes, Mayor Tabbshey looked down from his dais to see Terri, Georgia, Andie, and other Dominion players display an assortment of bumps and bruises. It appeared the kids were trying to display some sense of red mud rumble honor. Indeed, the Pirate Boys all appeared to have bumps and bruises too, but nothing serious. The mayor looked them over and shrugged. "This emergency meeting of the Belleville Town Council is called to order."

Teddy listened, as the mayor continued. "We are here tonight to discuss the 'Field Visitation Agreement.' So far, we have had a respectable red mud rumble, but we have not done much to keep our Belleville players focused on winning their championships for this town. Shoot, over coffee I heard someone complain, 'The Visitation Agreement has done more damage for this town than Old Luke ever did'."

"Honorable Mayor," LaFleur puffed, "I do believe sports in this town has given way to--"

"Hooliganism," interrupted Tabbshey with a smirk.

"What--?"

"I said 'hooliganism'. Mrs. Leavy said there was an emergency call about a brawl. Then I received a report from Deputy Measure. It was the 'Dominion Daughters Gang' who apparently invaded the Pirate's territory first and then--"

All took in a collective breath and looked on. Many expected the worst, until Mayor Tabbshey appeared to have a hard time holding a straight face. "And then I read in Measure's report that the rumble was perhaps the best seen around here the last twenty years."

"Why yes mayor," insisted Coach LaFleur. "Sir, it was terrible and--"

"I think 'invaded the Pirates' territory'," interrupted Coach Shimpock, "might be putting it a little strong and I--"

"Oh zip it you two." Mayor Tabbshey hammered down with his wood mallet. "Thank you both for your comments. That will be all I want to hear from either of you for the rest of this meeting."

As the Mayor conducted the towns other emergency business, no one seemed to listen. Voices got louder with disrespect for the mayor reduced by the minute. When it came time to revisit the Visitation Agreement, Teddy interrupted, "Hey everybody listen-up!"

Then Terri stepped forward and yelled at the top of her lungs, "Listen up!" The gallery quieted.

"Hear them out, mayor," Deputy Measure spoke, not worried about formality.

"What'll it be?" asked Mayor Tabbshey.

"Um," Teddy started. "My name is Teddy Fabiano. I am one of the *Fab 2*. I think we have only one person to blame for all this arguing over the field."

Those in the gallery grumbled accusations amongst themselves, as if to make anyone but themselves a target. Teddy pressed on. "So are we thinking no one here is to blame as long as it is not any one of us?" Teddy paused, looked around, and then continued. "When it gets rough we blame each other and suddenly it's not about our own responsibility? I mean, what kind of *Terrible Town Trauma* is this anyway? One minute we were laughing and the next thing it's like a major court-martial or something."

"We were actually having fun," continued Terri. "When y'all are not around and arguing, or stressed out we can actually have fun *and* be 'focused.' Does anyone understand why we were laughing?" asked Terri. "Why we wanted to laugh when we rumbled?"

"I can explain," said Attorney Litton.

Rising to interrupt, Nate waved off the attorney. "No way and with all respect due Attorney Litton, this will not be one of those deals where the lawyers get rich from some fancy story that gets more fantastic. I for one do not want, nor need another gloss-over of the real issues here."

"Not sure what you are getting at," the mayor wanted more from Nate.

"Mayor, Belleville has to have more character, more pride, and confidence than to--"

"Why yes, that would be correct," interrupted Tabbshey. "And, I like what you said and will be the first to--" He paused, and then smiled. "Yes Nate, I agree. From this time forward, I declare the Town of Belleville will have more pride and confidence. And by rickety tick, we are going to stop blaming anyone, or anything around here for our own poor behavior."

Nobby leaned over to Teddy and whispered, "Is this KEWL or what?"

"So what will we do to get this town right again?" asked Mayor Tabbshey. "What do we do to get everyone working together? Maybe even get back to the give and take of a little sportsmanship around here?"

"What about a friendly competition?" Coach LaFleur tried to offer something positive.

"A competition," Teddy's expression brightened, "some interesting potential for *Winner-Take-All Trauma* here."

"And the winner gets the 'final say' in what goes on with the Old Ballpark," added LaFleur.

"Ah for the love of--" snorted Coach Shimpock.

"Or," Teddy gulped, "maybe not so 'interesting'."

"That will be enough right there Shimpock," Mayor Tabbshey snapped. "Coach LaFleur, was there a suggestion you want to share?"

"Umm, not really," LaFleur stalled, "but you name it Mr. Mayor, and the Pirates will rise up, sabers drawn from scabbards to meet the challenge."

"Anything at all?"

"Yes, of course." Coach LaFleur continued. "The Pirates win and the town builds the Dominion their own soccer pitch before anything else. No sport, other than soccer will come first."

"And we lose and we look for a sand lot," lamented Spider.

"Oh no, *Silica Sand Lot Trauma*," whispered Teddy.

"Wait," cautioned Nobby. "I don't get it. What is a 'sand lot'?"

"No grass," answered Chris.

"Lots of ants," replied Teddy.

"And hot," added Spider.

Teddy in despair, raised his hands in the air. "It is like the *Rancho Cucamonga* of Little League, the Single 'A' for kid baseball."

"Then Cricket *would* be better?" Nobby calculated.

"Nobby," Teddy rolled his eyes skyward. "At this difficult time in the history of baseball, you bring up Cricket?"

"Order," declared Mayor Tabbshey. "Scratch the 'Field Visitation Agreement' and forget about the Cricket and Cucamonga or whatever. I no longer believe the Agreement is a great idea."

"Yep," Teddy smiled. "*Cucamonga Cricket Trauma* at its best."

"So instead of the Visitation Agreement," decreed the mayor, "we will have a challenge by the Pirates to compete head-on with the Dominion Daughters."

The gallery quieted to listen.

"Coach Shimpock of the Dominion Daughters and Coach LaFleur of the Little League Pirates, you will prepare your respective teams to compete against one another for the exclusive use of the Old 'B'."

"Exclusive use of what?" blurted Coach LaFleur.

Mayor Tabbshey looked down to pin the coaches where they stood. "The winner shall have the exclusive use of the Old 'B' until we can re-build the soccer pitches."

"But that means--" Coach LaFleur choked on her own words.

Shimpock smiled.

"That means *all or nothing*," said Mayor Tabbshey.

"So the kids in this town will play *either* soccer *or* baseball?" asked LaFleur, nervously.

"Should have been careful what you asked for," grinned the mayor. "Coach LaFleur, you and others in this community have taken the spirit of Belleville athletics, a most incredible legacy, and reduced it all to a flopper's nonsense wager. I will not be 'easy' about this," roared Tabbshey. The tips of his ears reddened. "I am here to avoid the destruction of the fine spirit of competition this town has fostered and nurtured throughout the many years of hard work and hard play exampled by our forefathers."

Nate nodded his head with approval, as he watched the mayor perform like a plate umpire who could not see through the dirt and dust during a play at the plate, but knew he had to *Sell-the-Call* regardless if the call was right or not. The gavel banged. "Let the record reflect there shall be a competition in Belleville to determine who of the Dominion and the Pirates shall win the Old 'B' home field advantage!"

Bewildered, both coaches looked on as Nate asked, "Mayor, what exactly will the teams have to do?"

"Oh, don't worry. No special equipment to order for this one."

"Actually," Nate questioned, "I was wondering what would be a fair sport to choose."

"'Fair sport'," the Mayor considered. "Well it would have to be a fair game of--" The mayor stalled to think, "I guess it will have to involve all team members and--"

"Running," volunteered Coach Shimpock.

"Throwing," added Coach LaFleur.

"Something that will involve the whole town," Nate agreed, inspired as the gallery hummed with anticipation.

"Nate?" asked Tabbshey.

"Yes," Nate approached to listen.

"Nate do you think you can come up with something?" The conversation fell to murmur as the mayor continued. "And what about something like--?"

The quiet conversation continued, until Nate volunteered for all to hear. "You are on to something good here. I believe we can have that ready for you in time, Mr. Mayor."

"Thank you." Mayor Tabbshey leaned back to study Nate's expression.

"I do believe the Town of Belleville will be a better place for it," said Nate.

"And getting after it on Founders' Day will prove it!" beamed Mayor Tabbshey.

Chapter 16

Round and Round

The next day, Nate spread the paper out and started to read. He and Teddy sat in the Old 'B' bleachers with Teddy listening as Nate read aloud, "*Mayor Tabbshey took the high road to defend the spirit of Belleville, rather than get lost in the legal wrangling.*" With a casual flip of the page, Nate continued. "*And so begins the preparation of Belleville for the Founders' Day Frisbee Marathon.*"

Nate folded the paper and leaned forward. "You know Teddy, I am not exactly sure what the rules are in a Frisbee Marathon, but the mayor said he would tell us something right after the Founders' Parade."

Teddy quipped, "Can't be many rules then."

Nate straightened, "Nothing like a little build-up and suspense. All I know is we will need a red Frisbee for the Dominion Daughters and a blue Frisbee for the Pirates."

"Should be interesting," said Teddy. "Why are we doing this anyway?"

"I'm thinking this town's challenge is to remain proud, optimistic about our sport legacy, and to get back to being all about *Belleville Strong.*"

Nate and Teddy looked down to the field and listened as the Dominion Daughters prepared for the Founders' Day Frisbee Marathon.

Teddy listened closely as down on the field, Coach Shimpock hollered, "Watch Kinny's timing for the catch of the long toss."

Andie ran up to Coach Shimpock. "How we doing, coach?"

"I am thinking our throws will be better if we relax and think about what we gotta' do," said Coach Shimpock. "Just remember participate and anticipate and then participate and anticipate and…."

"That's just all the same thing being said round and round," complained Terri.

"Round and round," Coach Shimpock smiled a Buddha's smile. "Just like the Frisbee in the air, round and round and round and--"

"You are kidding right?" whined Andie.

"Around and around and around," Coach Shimpock walked through the girls, the Frisbee held in the air and rotated in the coach's hands as if to hypnotize the players.

"He's lost it," Terri stared off into center field.

"I'm thinking we are caught up in something we have no clue about," Georgia warned.

"And that we don't want to do," Andie mumbled. "How can he coach us up for a Frisbee Marathon anyway?"

"I don't know," said Terri, "but we have to decide this instant, if we want to win this marathon--"

"Huh?"

"It's simple," Terri delivered her message. "We cannot win at this if we do not want to do it. We have to love what we are doing, if we are going to win back what we love."

"She's right," agreed Andie. The Dominion Daughters took their positions on the temporary soccer pitch. Coach Shimpock yelled, "Sharp now! Go long Terri!"

Terri reared back and then let the red Frisbee sail.

"That's it," called out Shimpock. "Good work Dom Dots!"

Kinny barked her approval. Her tail wagged cheerfully.

Deep in center field, Andie ran hard to catch the red Frisbee. She never lost sight of the flying discus as it sailed toward the wall. Closer, closer Andie suddenly took to the air. Her jump to catch the Frisbee was enough for her to grab at the discus, and she pulled it out of the air just in time to crash into the dark green barrier. Andie winced and gritted her teeth as she hit the wall hard. "Auggh!" A rush of wind left her lungs and gut. She crumpled to the ground, but still held the Frisbee. Her catch was good.

"Great catch Andie," coached Shimpock. "It's time for sprints!"

"Coach," complained Georgia. "Why do we have to run?"

"Whatever the contest," reasoned Shimpock, "we will always outrun the Pirates."

"But Coach," Terri protested, her on-the-field leadership put in question.

"Go," ordered Shimpock. "Hit it hard for a fast lap."

Quick to run a hot pace along the first base line, Terri headed along the Warning Track in right field. With a good dirt track to run on along the wall, Terri ran hard to set an example. She knew she had to earn her leadership back. As she turned left, she sprinted and her teammates joined her along the third base line.

"Let's do it," shouted Andie.

"Let's do this." Terri gritted her teeth.

"Dominion," yelled Georgia, as they all sprinted with a strong finish to home plate.

Terri stepped on the plate to the cheers of her teammates, and then walked back to stand on home plate with her teammates gathered around. With a glare into the eye of every teammate at the plate, Terri then closed her eyes to slits, despite the sun being at her back. Then she growled, "We can outrun 'em, outsmart 'em. We can beat those Pirates, but we won't!"

Gasps rose-up from her teammates.

"We won't?" Georgia cried aloud. "But why won't we win?"

"We won't," Terri raised her voice, "if we think we've won the marathon before we've tossed the first Frisbee!"

"Overconfidence," whispered Andie, the realization complete.

"Yes." Terri punched the air. "Overconfidence will defeat the Dominion before we even start!"

"So what do we do?" pleaded Georgia.

"There will be no sloppy Frisbee," rallied Terri. "No Sloppy Frisbee! No Sloppy Frisbee!"

Soon all heard the chant throughout the Old 'B' and beyond. As the Belleville Town Founders' placed American Flags in the sidewalks along Main Street, they listened, not sure what the Dominion chanted. With a collective shrug, they turned their attention back to their flags and red white and blue banners and streamers hoisted and secured high overhead. The wind danced with the welcome display, essential to the Founders' Day celebration, all that had to be considered was that before long, Belleville would once again be strong come the next morning's light.

Chapter 17

Frisbees and Planks

Now to practice for the marathon on the Old 'B' field, Teddy watched as the Pirates prepared. There was a Frisbee tossed between the first and third base lines, but no one was quite sure what to do. Coach LaFleur bellowed, "Pirates anticipate and do not merely participate!"

"Huh?" Tape shrugged, as Munch chewed noisily on his bat of choice, a Louisville Slugger as old as the Old 'B' itself.

"Anticipate what?" Teddy blurted. He caught the Frisbee coming toward home plate.

"The whole thing man," said Chris, intensely. "Everything man. Anticipate it all."

"That's right boys," Coach LaFleur encouraged. "Anticipate the course. Anticipate the rules. It is all about the anticipation of everything possible."

"You know 'everything' is secret until after the Parade," Tape was suspicious.

"You can anticipate the marathon takes place in this town," said Coach LaFleur.

"Yeah," agreed Spider.

"I get it," said Chris. "So how many places can this Frisbee Marathon go?"

"Exactly," volunteered Tape. "It won't go to the dog pound--"

"Or the car wash," said Teddy.

"Exactly wrong boys," argued Coach LaFleur. "Remember, 'anticipation.' I predict those are exactly the kind of places the marathon will go."

"Just the thought of running a marathon," Teddy cringed. "Why does the human race have to run at all? Why don't we all just agree to walk everywhere?"

"Hey, man," teased Chris. "Your *Bobo Reduction Program* you are always talking about? Don't you need to run to get rid of that belly of yours?"

"My Bobo Reduction Program definitely does not include a Frisbee Marathon."

"Boys," Coach LaFleur called out. "Get used to throwing the longer ones."

Teddy was uncomfortable, as he took a couple of steps backward. Spider looked over. "What's the matter, Reddy Teddy?"

"I dunno'." Teddy tossed the Frisbee. "Just feel like I'm walking the plank backwards or something."

"Walking the plank," Tape received the toss from Teddy. "I have never thought of losing that way."

"Are we going to kick some Dominion butt?" shouted Teddy, the call requiring a warrior-like response.

"Aye- aye captain," the Pirates hollered back.

"Do we walk *The Plank?*"

"No Plank today! No Plank today!"

"All right Pirates, get this Frisbee flying!" said Coach LaFleur. She handed the Frisbee to Teddy and he tossed it to Tape, who from first base flipped the blue discus to Nobby at second. Nobby flicked a short toss to Chris in deep center field. From Chris to Nobby, to Teddy at home plate. The practice continued, as Munch sported a mini-keg and red vest with "Munch's Marathon Power" written on it. After the dog ambled a little, he lay down in some shade for his pre Founders' Day Parade and Frisbee Marathon nap.

"How's it looking, coach?" asked Teddy.

"We all need to work on the long toss!"

"You mean run some more," Teddy gulped.

"Yes Teddy," smiled LaFleur. "And you go first."

"Where to coach?" asked Teddy.

"Go to the Main Street Gate and back," directed LaFleur. "We need you at your best today."

"I'll be exhausted," whined Teddy.

Coach LaFleur looked Teddy in the eye. "It will make you *Pirate Strong.*"

"Yes, coach." Teddy was not convinced.

"Do you want the Dominion to put the *Frisbee Wallop* on you today?" challenged Coach LaFleur.

"No coach," yelled Chris.

"No way," hollered Tape.

"Most certainly not," shouted Nobby.

"And you Teddy," LaFleur pressured, "you want to get Frisbee Walloped by the Dominion?"

"No, coach" Teddy jogged to the pitcher's mound, and then

reached second base where he stopped. Now the center of attention, Teddy turned back to face home plate, Coach LaFleur, and everyone in the Old "B." His eyes squinted, even though the sun was at his back. He sneered and looked around to see each one of the Pirates look to him for leadership. With a long, deep breath, Teddy said loud enough for everyone to hear, "There will be no Pirate here today, who will be Frisbee Walloped or walk the plank as long as I am the captain of this ship!"

"Yes!" Chris slapped his glove.

"Yeah man," crowed Spider. "That's what this Pirate is talkin' about."

"Arrr-B-Darrr," growled Tape.

All around him, the Pirates clapped, at first slowly, then faster as they gathered around Teddy at second base. Huddled, each player with hand toward the middle chanted, "No Wallop, No Plank! No Wallop, No Plank!" Soon Belleville filled with the chant from the Old "B." Did it sound crazy to those who prepared for the Founders' Day Parade and Marathon? "You bet," thought Teddy, "but that's what we need around here … a little crazy to get us going in the right directions."

Chapter 18

Float Preparation

After practice, Teddy wandered around by himself. He wanted a final look at the float preparation prior to the Founders' Day Parade. Alongside the Belleville Sport Store, Teddy heard Nate whistle, and then watched as he pulled a red Frisbee and stapled it to his *Counter of Success* float. Then Nate pulled a blue one to layer over the red and stapled it over with a white discus. Teddy smiled, as soon there appeared a swooping Frisbee bunting on the Counter of Success featured high in the middle of the float.

Content, Teddy wandered over to the parking lot at City Hall. There he watched as float builders worked the final additions on *The Spirit of Belleville*. Mayor Tabbshey smiled proudly from under his handlebar mustache and crowed, "She is a beauty! Say, what are those two big green things over there?"

"Those are two grass playing fields coming together," explained a float builder.

"But they look like they are coming apart." The mayor was concerned. "We do not want any suggestion of a '*come-a-part*' around here."

"We'll work on that, Mr. Mayor."

"Hey mayor," Nate hollered from across the alley. "I like the way your float looks like the community is coming together."

Mayor Tabbshey looked over, surprised. "It looks good from back there?"

"Sure thing," Nate called out and waved.

The Mayor looked again at The Spirit of Belleville float and volunteered, "You hear that? Mr. Nate Abelard says it looks like the community is coming together."

"Sounds good mayor," said the float builder. "Oh and thanks."

"Well you know a well-deserved compliment can always be heard by the well-deserved."

"What's that?" asked the float builder, busy again with the final changes.

"Oh I was just saying 'well-deserved'," Mayor Tabbshey smiled.

"Yes, mayor, we got that."

Chapter 19

Patrolling the Parade

It was Founders' Day, and the start of the Belleville Founders' Day Parade that was at the Adams Mountain End of Main Street. After resting in the park, Teddy walked up Main Street and joined the rest of the team on the Pirate's "Run for More" Float. When he looked up toward the Adams Mountain Highway, he could make out Deputy Measure's patrol unit driving slowly through the switchbacks. Teddy then looked around and the marching band started to form columns of players with their instruments. Other parade floats like the bright green Gunderson's Groceries float, and the Caleb's Tire float staged, as they appeared ready to roll. Still other floats moved gracefully to park in line for the parade. From a distance, Teddy saw the empty Dominion Daughters float go by and from where he stood high on the Pirate float, it looked like one of the best entrants.

Teddy looked back to see Deputy Measure gazing through field glasses from high up Adam's Mountain. He figured the deputy's steely gaze locked right on through Main Street, and all the way to the parking lot at the Old "B." Teddy's attention was drawn back to the float staging area, where Nate's 'Counter of Success,' Belleville's' 'Spirit of Competition,' and the loaf-like 'Top Hat Bakery' floats cruised into position.

"Will you look at that," Teddy admired the bright green 'Gunderson's Groceries' float as it parked just behind the Pirate's float. Then Teddy noticed the Dominion Daughters float as it got nearer with its 'When it's Stop, it's Hands Off' message. A message for every teen in town to respect one another if they were thinking of interacting, perhaps hoping for someone to say 'yes' to more than friendship.

Now back in his police car, Deputy Measure drove up the Adam's Mountain Highway and Teddy figured the deputy would park in his favorite place. He knew how the deputy would position his car to monitor the speed of motorists who would dare drive brakeless, witless down Adam's Mountain. The mission today would be to protect the parade route. Ordered by Chief Flavio to slow everyone down, Teddy knew Deputy Measure was glad to be of service to his community.

As Teddy relaxed, the town folk and spectators from the city settled along Main Street. They set up their unfolded chairs and placed their brightly colored coolers and blankets all around the alternating Nation's and Founders' Flags.

Cooled by the breeze that drifted up and then flowed down Adam's Mountain, the adults talked and waited for the parade to begin. Most children scurried to play up and down the closed street. It was a kid's adventure to goof around along any closed parade route.

Teddy listened as a little girl held a soccer ball up against the belly of her expectant mother and giggled, "Sosher-ball, Mama."

"Oh no," Teddy cringed, "another lost generation."

"That is right," the expectant mother smiled. "Soccer--" Suddenly, the expectant mother reared and reached for her swollen belly. "He kicked."

"Sosher ... sosher," said the little girl.

After a while, Nate walked up to the Pirate Float and smiled up to offer, "It will be a great day to consider what got us here, and to get everything else sorted out around here."

"Man, I hope this town doesn't forget about baseball," Teddy replied.

"You know," Nate eyed Teddy carefully, "I seriously doubt you will let that happen."

"Oh." Teddy was not sure what else to say.

"It's great that your thoughts are of both this town's past, and the future generations of this prized sport town to come. But you know what?"

"What?"

"I happen to know that the mayor is as concerned, and hopes that this celebration and competition is going to help a lot of folks re-set their thinking from Old Luke mess."

"Can't we do both?" asked Teddy.

"That is what we are hoping for young man," Nate replied. "That is what we are hoping and praying for, young fella'."

Chapter 20

A Parade with No Brakes

Teddy watched as Nate walked on and made his way to the Grand Marshal's stage. There, he stood next to Mayor Tabbshey, who stood puffed proud like a content bullfrog.

The town's people and spectators from the city politely clapped, when the mayor approached the microphone. "Happy Founders' Day to all," Tabbshey's voice blasted through the karaoke speaker mounted on the back of a nearby golf cart. "I am proud to introduce to you this year's Grand Marshal, Mr. Nate Abelard of the Belleville Sport Store!"

"Thank you, good mayor."

"And thank you Grand Marshal Nate, not only the owner of the Belleville Sports Store, a sponsor of the 'Counter of Success' float and the Founders' day Frisbee Marathon … oh and by- the-way, this guy won the 'Best Float in Belleville' contest only moments ago."

Nate received the microphone from the mayor, and politely nodded away for the mentioning.

"I am certain you all will see many fine floats in today's Founders' Day Parade. We do welcome you to have the very best of fun today."

At the mention of 'fun,' the crowd cheered, hooted, and hollered.

"So let's get this parade on the road!"

The mayor and Nate hurried from the stage and crammed into the chauffeured golf cart.

"A golf-cart made for driving four around," the mayor giggled. "Get it?"

Nate looked at him a little confused.

"You know, made for four … and they holler 'Fore!' when a ball is driving toward someone."

"I do believe that would be a double pun, mayor," Nate corrected.

"Oh I guess you are right. I'd better correct my score card then."

"Very funny," Nate smiled.

"Thanks. Nate. I get to babbling and--"

Nate nodded and smiled as the cart jerked forward. The mayor was distracted as he waved and continued with his welcome of the spectators, "So good morning, Belleville. Not only is this day a celebration of our Founders' and their independence and character, but this day is also one of competition enough to prove how we can again use our freedoms to improve and find new ways to resolve our challenges and differences! I am proud to announce today's parade will be followed by the 'First Annual Belleville Founders' Day Frisbee Marathon'! So after the parade, please come to the parking lot at the Old 'B,' where the floats will be on display. You will also find the start line for the Founders' Day Frisbee Marathon."

Moments later, Teddy looked on as the cart driver dropped the mayor at the "Town's Spirit of Competition" float, and then dropped Nate at the "Counter of Success" float. As the mayor and Nate took their positions, the drum major for the Belleville High School Marching Band ordered, "Corps, Ten Hut!" The band snapped to attention, as Mayor Tabbshey looked on proudly.

Then the drum major ordered, "Horns Up!"

As the drum-line rapped a snappy march cadence, the drum major marched in place and gave the final order. "Ready ... Parade march!"

With a boom of base drums, the crash of mighty symbols, the band advanced as one onto the parade route. They played the "Theme from Superman" as the "Spirit of Competition" float followed. Mayor Tabbshey waved and greeted all the parade watchers.

Later, all the players and Baseball Mommies aboard the "Pirate Float" hollered and waved as the Pirates passed in front of the Belleville Sports Store. Then the "Counter of Success" float passed along with clowns throwing colorful Frisbees everywhere. Sometimes, when the parade backed up, the clowns played catch with the willing children and spectators along the parade route. Behind the Counter of Success, the Soccer Tommies rode the "Dominion Daughters float", waved, and cheered to their friends and families. An Appaloosa riding demonstration followed, as Main Street filled with good cheer and celebration.

The parade finished at the Old 'B' parking lot. Teddy watched from the Pirate's float as the marching band rested, while vehicles and floats continued to park. Owners hitched up their horses, as sirens wailed and horns zonked to signal the close of the parade. As was also tradition, the spectators and parade participants began to walk toward and around the static display of floats. As they gathered, there was talk of picnicking with family and friends.

Teddy looked back, and toward Adam's Mountain to again see Deputy Measure alert as he watched over the town. The wail of sirens and horn blasts from the fire trucks, police cars, and ambulances signaled the end of the Founders' Day Parade. Teddy looked away, he could not possibly have heard Deputy Measure mutter, "Over for another year," but Teddy felt that Deputy Measure wished he could have been a part of the parade. Then, for no reason he could explain, Teddy looked up and saw a large truck speed brakeless, witless down the Adam's Mountain Highway. Teddy watched carefully, as Measure coolly got into his unit and prepared for the chase down.

As Teddy learned from Deputy Measure after all was said-and-done, he communicated to dispatch, "Mrs. Leavy. We got a fast one here."

"Roger that," acknowledged Mrs. Leavy at radio dispatch. "Hooligans," she snapped. "I'll let Chief Flavio know."

With the radio microphone still open, Mrs. Leavy could hear the truck race past and the driver in the "Fuller's Brakes & Auto Supply" truck scream, "Help me!"

Teddy looked on in horror as the truck sped out of control and down Adam's Mountain.

"He's headed this way," Teddy growled as he saw the lights and heard the siren from Measure's police car. However, the siren quickly blended with the parade sirens that seemed to go on longer than usual.

Teddy made a quick survey of the situation in the Old 'B' parking lot. It remained full of happy spectators, who hollered for the driver of the Belleville E-1 fire engine to continue her siren, and to extend the parade celebration. Teddy knew that Deputy Measure had to chase the Fuller's Brake Truck down Adam's Mountain, and that they would head straight down Main Street if the chase continued. Teddy knew he had to make a difference, just as much as Deputy Measure's duty was to stop the out-of-control truck.

The Fuller's truck sped onto Main Street at high speed. The decision of Deputy Measure was to drive his police car faster, and with all his skill pull past it far enough to head off the deadly truck. Measure knew he had to stop it before it reached the Old "B." parking area.

Driving intensely, Measure's police car blasted the only siren now heard in Belleville. He caught up to the Fuller's truck and tried to pull alongside, but there was not enough room to maneuver alongside safely.

At the parking lot of the Old "B," firefighter Jess hopped down from the E-1 fire engine. Teddy called out as he ran toward her, "Get everyone away from Main Street!"

"That siren," Jess looked down at Kinny. Without a command, Kinny began to bark and nip at everyone's heels to warn as many spectators as possible.

Teddy joined Jess and they hurried alongside the fire engine. "Measure is trying to get alongside," Teddy whispered hoarsely. The lone siren was growing faster and louder. "That truck is headed straight for us," exclaimed Teddy. "The driver has lost control!"

With a quick spin, Jess scrambled to the top of the E-1 fire truck as Kinny herded more and more people away from the Old 'B' parking lot. Kinny drove them into the open areas not filled with Old Luke tornado-junk.

From on top of the E-1 Jess yelled, "This is an emergency! Everyone run to the park. Get away from Main Street. Run to the park!"

"Get behind a car," yelled Teddy to the expectant mother and the little "Sosher Girl."

"Get behind a truck," commanded Jess. "Get behind anything big if you can't run. There's a runaway truck!"

Munch howled his alert, as Kinny herded more and more families to safety.

People looked around in confusion. Teddy, Kinny, Munch, and the other firefighters did their best to direct people to safety before the Fuller's Brake Truck crashed into the Old "B." Only blocks from certain disaster, the Fuller truck appeared closer and closer. Teddy watched, careful not to panic as Measure again tried to get his police car around the truck. He could not. Instead, Measure crashed into the side of the truck, but the contact did not slow the truck that closed fast on the unprotected people.

Teddy looked on as Measure fought as hard as possible to inch his battered police car ahead. With gritted teeth, Measure knew he would have only one more chance to make a difference and save lives.

Chapter 21

The Measure of Hero

Teddy could see Deputy Measure steer his police car out and to the side of the run-a-way Fuller truck. Then the police car pulled even with heavy contact until Measure cleared the speeding truck's bumper, like a NASCAR driver taking first place with a high-speed dive and swoop.

"He's gonna' block it," Teddy yelled; his voice was raw.

The police car, with Deputy Measure driving, began to swerve back and forth. At the same time, the car slowed to try to make contact and stop the truck using the brakes of the police car.

"Come on," Teddy whispered. "Deputy Measure you can let him run into you and then you can use your brakes. Hold on tight. Come on. Slow down."

It looked like Measure was using his car to slow the Fuller's Truck. "He's blocking the truck," cheered Teddy.

Then it appeared the police car did not slow the truck fast enough. The car positioned square in front of the truck as Deputy Measure stepped on the car brakes, but the truck was much larger and heavier. The smaller police car could not slow the larger truck fast enough. Teddy realized there was not enough time to battle the truck to a gradual stop.

"I hope he has another idea," said Teddy.

Deputy Measure waited for the truck to ram again and when it did, he stepped hard on the emergency brake of the police car. Doing so caused the back end of his car to break loose and drift left. With the vehicles locked up, Measure's police car took the front end of the Fuller's truck with him and away from the path toward the frightened people.

The Fuller truck's new course was straight toward the Counter of Success float, now an isolated island in the middle of the Old 'B' parking lot. In an instant, Measure's police car swerved to avoid the Counter of Success, and crashed into a green dumpster. Trash exploded everywhere from the booming impact of the car and metal trash box, "Barroomf!" Measure's car smashed to rest and all went silent around him, except for the rush of steam from his destroyed radiator.

Then the Fuller's truck swerved and slammed into the Counter of Success float, "Shawump!"

Pieces of red, white, and blue Frisbees flew everywhere. Chunks of paper mache hurtled through the air like missiles. A white Frisbee caught Kinny in the ribs. She took the blow and staggered as she struggled for breath.

All went strangely quiet.

The lawn sprinklers slowly rose and sputtered to a strange life throughout the surrounding park areas and baseball diamond. It was hard to tell the hiss of radiators from the sprinklers.

Wounded and unnoticed in the confusion, Kinny made her way through the Main Street Gate. She hobbled through the relentless sprinklers and toward the empty visitors' dugout.

Jess the firefighter and Teddy were closest to the truck. Jess dashed to the scene, a mess of banners, broken decorations, and truck parts that read like a busted-up billboard, 'COUNT O' SUCCESSFUL BRAKES.'

"I'm going to check on Deputy Measure," Teddy shouted. The police and other brave first responders rushed to the scene. Engaged in rescue operations within seconds, there was no panic until Mayor Tabbshey and Nate came out from their crouched positions behind the Spirit of Belleville float. The hosts of the day's event looked on in silent shock. Chief Flavio, his belt low under his belly, approached Eddie, the driver of the wrecked Fuller's truck. "Edward you drunk?" demanded Chief Flavio.

The nervous driver replied, "No chief. The brakes went bad. I couldn't--"

"We'll take that as a 'yes'." Chief took Eddie by the arms and twisted them to cuff his hands behind his back. "You are under arrest for driving under the influence and reckless endangerment. Anything you say can and will be used against you--"

"But Chief?"

"Run 'em in," Chief Flavio ordered, as he passed the cuffed man onto another deputy. "Get him to the hospital. I want a blood test and have him checked out." Flavio turned with all attention to his downed Deputy Measure. "We haven't got time to waste. I gotta get over to Measure."

Mayor Tabbshey growled, "That lowdown scoundrel deserves a good kick by a jackass."

"You the one to do it?" asked the chief.

"Mayor, we have a man down," interrupted Nate. "This is not the time."

Deputy Measure lay unconscious. His head rolled back as the emergency medical technicians and firefighters fought to open the car door with the *Jaws of Life*. The firefighters and emergency medical technicians pulled Measure's limp figure out of the car. They carefully loaded him on a backboard.

"Teddy," Terri ran up to Teddy, panicky. "You see Kinny anywhere?"

"No," Teddy responded, his thoughts elsewhere. "Is Deputy Measure okay?"

"He's unconscious," Terri whimpered. "I saw blood on the door."

The ambulance doors slammed shut, and the siren wailed as it drove off. Mayor Tabbshey stood before the destroyed combination of cars, floats, and trucks, as Attorney Litton, Coach LaFleur, and Coach Shimpock joined the group. The Pirates and the Dominion Daughters followed their coaches and moved on close to listen. Nate looked through the crowd, puzzled when he did not see the Fab 2. After a moment of idle conversation, Mayor Tabbshey turned to Litton. "I believe we have a hero who needs this town's prayers and concern."

"Agreed," murmured Litton.

Coach Shimpock and Coach LaFleur listened closely, and then Shimpock said, "We can do the marathon another time."

"Don't you think Deputy Measure would want the town to continue?" Coach LaFleur clicked and flicked her long, red, white, and blue fingernails.

"Jeez Marcie," snarled Mayor Tabbshey. "Do you ever give it a rest?"

"Mayor, I have never seen you snarl before," Nate remarked.

"Well maybe that's what we need around here," Mayor Tabbshey snarled some more. "Y'all need a good measure of 'snarl' to keep things real."

Chapter 22

The Marathon Must Run On

Teddy knew that Belleville was again to endure another disaster. He looked on as some folks tried to provide support, while others needed the care. People huddled around the Spirit of Belleville float, and listened as Coach Shimpock encouraged, "Listen Dom-Dots we have to rally and provide support for--"

"Shimpock is right," interrupted Attorney Litton. "The marathon can wait."

Teddy looked on, as Mayor Tabbshey glanced at Nate. Then they all looked toward the Adam's Mountain end of Main Street where some folks picked up belongings dropped during the scramble for safety. Others looked for things that were just lost. Still others headed for their cars. They just wanted to put distance between them and the latest Belleville tragedy. Then the mayor saw Grandma McIvor. "G-McMa is going home."

All looked on as G-McMa walked slowly, her head hung low. She went straight up onto her dark, empty looking porch and sat. She just sat, looking off toward Adam's Mountain.

"This was the first time G-McMa ventured off her porch since Old Luke," said the mayor.

"It will probably be weeks before she again sets a foot in the sun," guessed Litton.

As he thought about such things, the mayor heard the slap of running shoes approach. Some looked up, while others remained disinterested. Then Terri came into full view. She ran hard down Main Street. "Everybody," yelled Terri. "Hey mayor he'll be all right!"

"He'll be alright," Terri repeated the news, as she ran right into the mayor and bounced off his belly and into the arms of a startled Coach Shimpock. "I followed the ambulance to the hospital and watched Deputy Measure climb out. Jess the firefighter, gave me the thumbs up!"

"So he will be okay?" Mayor Tabbshey was eager to hear the good news.

"Wait," cautioned Litton. "He's not out of the woods yet."

"So maybe we ought to celebrate our new hero?" suggested Tabbshey.

"We need to hear from the doctors first," warned Nate. "Mayor, do not push things now."

"But these people need to celebrate something!"

"So we name the marathon after Al," suggested Litton.

"Exactly, that will do it!"

Mayor Tabbshey quickly climbed up on the Spirit of Belleville float and announced to everyone, "Belleville line up for 'The Al Measure Founders' Day Frisbee Marathon'!"

Some looked up, bewildered. Some wondered aloud, "Has the mayor finally lost all his marbles?"

"C'mon, people. Let's get this Frisbee Marathon flying!" Mayor Tabbshey climbed down from the float to lead the willing forward. Teddy looked on, his breath still deep and forced, as many joined their *Pied Piper* Mayor. "I guess we just go along with it," said Teddy. "It sounds positive, and I'm all in for anything that will be good for this town right about now."

Chapter 23

There will still be a Marathon

Teddy joined in and moved forward with the flow of the crowd as they passed through the Main Street Gate. Once on the Old 'B' outfield, Mayor Tabbshey marched through the sprinklers and toward the ball diamond. The willing crowd followed, as he directed the Pirate team to line up on the first base line. The Dominion Daughters lined up on the third base side.

Teddy thought he saw Kinny peek out of the visitor's dugout, but was not sure. No one else seemed to notice the injured dog. Teddy's attention shifted to the emboldened mayor, who handed a secret marathon map to a surprised Coach LaFleur. Then a confident Coach Shimpock received the Dominion's copy. "The marathon rules and maps," Teddy whispered.

"Ah hem," Mayor Tabbshey spoke aloud. "Each coach will call out the commands, step-by-step. Each call-out must include the player chosen to throw, and the name of the second player to catch the Frisbee in their locations that are determined on the map."

With a listen from the first base line, Teddy looked straight ahead and adjusted his cap with authority. Tape also listened, and then carefully whispered to Teddy, "You ready, Teddy?"

"He is kidding, right?" grumbled Teddy. "I mean running and listening to the coaches and all that stuff?"

"Isn't that what we are always supposed to do?" asked Tape.

Teddy just frowned. "We'll get this thing done."

"May the best team win," hollered Mayor Tabbshey, his swagger nervous. "May the team that is best, win as well."

Teddy looked over to the third base line, where Terri pranced in place. He could hear her as she spoke to Andie. "We're going to really embarrass those *Nine Inning Ninnies*."

"I'll settle for a clean victory," commented Andie, coolly.

"You would 'settle'?" challenged Terri. "Why 'settle' when you can select victory *and* total domination over the Pirates?"

Andie appeared unsure as Terri looked toward the first base line, where Teddy watched. It was then, she saw Teddy turn slowly to square up with her. His eyes squinted wicked into the sun as she shouted, "I hear there's a lot of running in a marathon."

"Oh, you think so." Teddy's comebacker was not as strong as it could have been. Then he decided he would not to be outdone and hollered, "Tell us more about your party with the little itty-bitty skunksters little--"

"No," Spider gasped. "Don't agitate the Dom Dots."

"Sister--"

"No!" shouted Tape, "Not the 'little sister' bomb!"

"My friends," Teddy did not glance over, "there will be no tidy victories today."

As if on cue, Teddy received a sinister smile from Terri, and then she called out, "It's 'Game On' little Brudder." Terri placed her foot down, to assume an aggressive stance, her steely concentration on the first base line unmistakable. Teddy gulped a dry gulp, because there was no spit to spit. He thought the skunkster response would have been tough enough, but it was not and it was now marathon time ... and everyone knew there would be a lot of running.

Mayor Tabbshey placed the blue Pirate and the red Dominion Frisbees flat on home plate. Then Tabbshey raised his arms high in the air. "On your marks..."

Coaches LaFleur and Shimpock glared at one another, settled and readied for the start.

"Get set..."

Coach LaFleur dashed from third, and to home plate.

Then Mayor Tabbshey shouted, "Go!"

Along the first base line, Coach Shimpock waited, and then saw LaFleur's early move.

"She cheated," crowed Shimpock.

"Play on coach Shimpock," encouraged Terri.

Teddy watched in horror as Shimpock caught up to LaFleur, all advantage lost as Shimpock grabbed the red Frisbee.

"Terri catches at first base!"

Terri scrambled from the third base line, across the pitcher's mound to first base.

"Tape to first base," shouted LaFleur.

Tape took a couple of steps and was on the first base bag.

Shimpock threw the red discus in the air to where Terri was expected.

Marty took a couple of steps toward first base, and looked for the blue Frisbee to fly toward him.

"Terri, toss to Andie at third base," shouted Shimpock.

"Here," LaFleur handed the blue Frisbee to Teddy. "You throw it." Teddy threw the blue Frisbee to Tape at first base. After throws to third base, where Spider and Andie waited, the crowd cheered and the "Al Measure Founders Day Frisbee Marathon" was off to a flying start.

From the visitor's dugout, Kinny peaked out and whimpered. The mascot was not happy, because she could not chase the red Frisbee for her team. The crowd cheered, as Georgia received her toss from Andie.

"To the Main Street Gate," Coach Shimpock shouted. "Throw as far as you can!"

The teams sprinted across the field and toward the Main Street Gate.

"Spider to Nobby," directed Coach LaFleur. Spider threw the blue Frisbee, but it was too low and did not carry.

Nobby ran hard and dove to snag the low flying Frisbee before it landed in the grass. With a roll and a tumble, Nobby righted himself, popped up, and thrust the Frisbee high into the air. The Pirates and fans cheered.

Chris and Munch were at the Main Street Gate, bewildered. Coach LaFleur looked around, embarrassed and gave another order. "Throw to Chris at the Gate!"

Teddy looked on, and ran hard as the crowd jogged along with the mayor and through the Main Street Gate to the Old 'B' parking lot. Many could not see Kinny, now a stowaway on the mayor's cart. She peeked out from under a tarp used to cover the Karaoke speaker. Tabbshey announced, "Everyone please be very careful out here." The blast of sound caused Kinny to duck back under the tarp. "Be very, very careful as we all compete in Al's Founders' Day Marathon!"

Chapter 24

Car Wash Frisbee Football

Teddy jogged alongside the mayor and his enthusiastic followers. They made their way through the Old 'B' parking lot, where Tabbshey paused to call out, "Here's the score!"

"There is a score?" questioned Coach LaFleur.

"One to nothing," the mayor called out.

"I guess," Coach Shimpock shrugged. "Who has the one?"

"Because the Dominion Daughters have one dropped Frisbee," the mayor explained, "the score is Pirates 1 and the Dominion Daughters 0."

"Ohhh I get it," nodded Nobby. "It's kind of like Cricket."

"Really," Chris gave Nobby the *Stink Eye.* "You're still talking 'Cricket'?"

Mayor Tabbshey led on through the mostly empty parking lot. He drove the cart past the heaped piles of tornado-junk, along the line of floats and past Deputy Measure's crash site. Teddy looked on, as the sudden movement of a police car drew his attention. It pulled across and blocked the mayor's path. Chief Flavio climbed out of the car and walked toward the mayor's golf cart. "Bad news," said the chief.

"Let's have it." Mayor Tabbshey gripped the steering wheel.

"Deputy Measure collapsed," Chief Flavio shook his head sadly. "He's unconscious again."

"My God," the mayor dropped his head.

"They're doing tests, scans, and stuff."

The mayor called out, "Everybody stop this marathon."

"Why?" demanded Andie.

"Deputy Measure fell into a coma."

The crowd grew still, hushed.

"So we stop here," said Terri. "We quit?"

"Wait," Teddy tried to understand. "Deputy Measure's job was to make Main Street safe for us, right?"

"Right," said Terri.

"Shouldn't we use Main Street like it was intended?" asked Teddy.

"He will know it's for him," Nate said quietly.

"You're serious?" The mayor looked from face to face. "We get Al feeling good by still running this marathon?"

Coach Shimpock nodded. "Andie hit Terri!"

Terri bolted onto Main Street, where she glanced off the Dominion Float and caught her red Frisbee.

"Go Tape," ordered Coach LaFleur.

"This one's for Al's Marathon," Tape whooped and amped it up. His momentum quickly carried him too close to the bright green Gunderson's Grocery float.

"Oh no," Tape yowled and then collided. "Ugh!"

Green and gold float decorations flew everywhere. For some, the impact was a reminder of the accident earlier in the day. Silence settled over the crowd as Tape disappeared in the mess of grocery-like streamers and ribbons until the blue Frisbee punched out of the mess with an unexpected salute of victory.

"For my dad ... the Measure of a hero!" called out Tape.

The crowd cheered, and broke into a collective trot as an all-new parade of marathon fans formed behind Mayor Tabbshey's golf cart.

"Hey Tape?" asked Teddy. "Why aren't you in the hospital with your dad?"

"I'm too young to go in," explained Tape. "Besides, I agree with y'all. It's what he would want us to do."

Teddy listened as Coach LaFleur called out, "Teddy into the car wash." Coach LaFleur ticked and clicked her fingernails from finger to finger, one by one, a most definite tic, tic-rickety-tic.

"I need a volunteer to go into the Beautiful Car Wash with Teddy," called out Coach Shimpock.

"I'll go sir," replied Georgia.

"God Bless you," Coach Shimpock joked. "Thank you for taking one for the Dom Dots."

"For the Dominion, sir," said Georgia as she disappeared into the wash tunnel and looked for the Frisbee flying true between the drooping blue brushes.

Still at the entrance, Coach LaFleur stomped defiantly with her arms crossed. "Georgia is already in there. Teddy we need you to go in there and get it done!"

"All right already." Teddy gritted his teeth, lowered his head, and charged as if an enraged bull. With head lowered, Teddy ran about ten steps, only to plow into a big blue brush. He bounced straight back and landed hard on his butt. "Oh man," Teddy winced, "talk about the *Wrong Wash Cycle Trauma!*"

Georgia grinned mischievously as she hit the wash 'Start Button.' Then she dashed out, ahead of the water spray and the brushes that started to swirl. Teddy's howl from deep within the car wash tunnel soon muffled, as the car wash filled with water spray, soap and the sounds of motors and spinning blue brushes.

"Don't forget to wash behind your ears," Georgia giggled.

Through the water and brushes, Teddy popped up like a fullback with the blue discus tucked under his arm and dashed through the spitting, soapy water. "I'll get y'all," Teddy vowed as he dodged spray and made it past the churning blue brushes.

"I didn't know Teddy played football," said Tape.

"Best moves I've ever seen him make," grinned Spider.

Suddenly, Teddy exploded out the other end of the car wash with the Pirate yell, "Arrr-B-Darrr!"

"To the hospital," hollered Coach LaFleur.

"To the hospital," Coach Shimpock directed the Dominion.

It was not long before everyone got back into the rhythm of the marathon. With a sense about some good things to come, Kinny peeked out from under the tarp longingly. She wanted to be in the game, play hard, and to help the Dominion Daughters win the Old 'B' home field advantage.

Chapter 25

Hoo-ah Only During Visitors' Hours

Teddy recovered from the Frisbee car wash fiasco. Not entirely washed out, he remained alert and observed Tape and Georgia jostle at the hospital stairs. Looking skyward, Teddy followed his toss until Tape grabbed for the red Dominion Frisbee.

"No," Teddy moaned as Georgia pulled in the blue Pirate's Frisbee.

Only Teddy, Tape, and Georgia seemed to notice the mix-up as they hid the Frisbees behind their backs. Mayor Tabbshey announced, "Pirates 2 ... Dominion 1!"

Kinny cringed, as the karaoke speaker blared next to her delicate puppy ears.

Teddy watched as Tape and Georgia slyly took advantage of the distraction to exchange their discus. Then they hugged.

"Nice," Teddy mumbled as he kicked at the ground. "Now there goes a Pirate getting all mooshy gooshy with a Soccer Tommy."

Tape just looked over at Teddy, smiled, and shrugged.

Teddy could not help but be displeased with this turn of events.

"To the hospital door," Shimpock directed.

Andie charged hard through the automatic doors that opened and lead to the hospital hallway. Nobby followed and scurried through the doors and into the same hallway where an orderly named Samuel wheeled a chair with Mr. Cott, an elderly passenger riding along happily. With a gold Olympic medal around his neck, Mr. Cott let everyone know he was a Track and Field Olympian. He proudly wore his medal wherever he went. Mr. Cott looked up with a smile from ear to ear. "The marathon is here!"

"Easy Pops," said Samuel. "You're not competing in this one."

"But I always appreciate strong competition."

"I know you do. I know you do."

Not knowing what was going on in the Intensive Care Unit, Terri, Andie, and Georgia exchanged looks. "Let's let Deputy Measure know the Dominion Daughters are here for him."

The Dominion Daughters all smiled and chanted, "Get Well Al. Get Well Al. Get Well Al!"

Coach Shimpock turned to the Dominion Daughters and smiled, proudly, "Hooah Dom Dots. Outstanding … your performance is simply outstanding!"

Now on their way to the Belleville Pound, the Dominion Daughters shouted, "Heard, understood, and acknowledged, sir!"

"To the pound," Shimpock called.

"And then back to the Old 'B'," hollered Coach LaFleur.

The Dominion Daughters snarled and the Pirates cowered with a few 'Arrr-b-darrrs' heard just as Mayor Tabbshey shouted the latest score. "It's the Pirates 2 and the Dominion Daughters 2!"

"It's a tie?" Coach LaFleur clicked her nails nervously.

"What the heck?" Coach Shimpock puzzled.

Teddy whined, "It's the craziest scoring ever."

At the Belleville Pound, excited dogs grew louder, as Karlee flipped the red Frisbee to Georgia and the coaches and teammates flowed into the large kennel-lined cave. Georgia, distracted by the sounds of barking dogs, stopped and listened.

Tape's attention was also on the kenneled dogs. He started to wander, confused. He had heard about the pound, and was participating in this world for the first time.

After a few moments, Coach LaFleur demanded, "Where's Tape? He's supposed to be throwing the Frisbee to--"

"Don't know," said Chris.

Nobby saw Tape kneeled before a kennel, with a Pug pressed up to the kennel grate. There were tears in Tape's eyes.

"He's over here," Nobby reported, and then yelled over to Tape. "C'mon man. We gotta' win this marathon."

Tape stood halfheartedly, his arm cocked to throw the Frisbee. All the dogs got quiet, as they concentrated on the Frisbee. Tape smiled, because there was not a critter without full attention on the Frisbee.

"Are they are Frisbee dogs?" asked Chris.

Everyone in the pound stopped when all the dogs went silent. Only Andie took advantage of the pause to throw the red Frisbee through the door and into the waiting hands of Terri.

Tape moved to throw his Frisbee, and when he did all the dogs chased the Frisbee from inside their kennels. Suddenly, there was a huge 'Blam' followed by all kinds of barking and yipping. Unfortunately, the dogs all plowed into the sides of their kennels.

The yips and yowls were deafening, but Chris did not care. "You see that?" he marveled. "They are all Frisbee dogs!"

"I'll be back for one," Tape vowed.

"You want to adopt one?" puzzled Chris, as Teddy looked on with a smile.

"I want to adopt them all," cried Tape as he threw the Frisbee to Chris.

After going through the dog pound, Teddy and all participants raced back along Main Street, and through the Old 'B' Gate. It was then they saw the two soccer goals positioned in right and left field. "What the heck?" Teddy demanded.

"You know," said Spider, "those soccer nets just don't look any good on the baseball field."

As the crowd readied for the final moments of the marathon, the energy was positive. Everyone knew it was time to decide the important matter of home field advantage at the Old "B."

Coach Shimpock commanded, "Terri take the goal at the south end!"

Coach LaFleur called out, "Teddy to the goal at the north end!"

Frustrated, Teddy jogged to the goal. He knew he was about to cross over to the dark, soccer side. With a shrug, Chris launched the blue Frisbee high into the air.

Kinny peeked out from underneath the tarp. She still wished she could chase and intercept that high-flying blue bird of a Frisbee.

"Terri, let her fly," encouraged Coach Shimpock. "Dominion, go and finish these Pirates!"

"Whoot … Whoot," the Dom Dots cheered and jumped.

Teddy looked on, not at all happy about the developments. "Pirates," Coach LaFleur called in her team. "It's time to take back your Old 'B'."

"Arrr-B-Darrr," cheered the Pirates. Some slashed at the wind with their air-sabers.

LaFleur directed, "Teddy to Eric at second base and Nobby to the pitcher's mound!"

"Terri to Georgia, then back to Terri at the pitcher's mound," yelled Coach Shimpock.

The mayor sped toward them all, as Kinny peeked from under the tarp.

"This the way it is supposed to end, Mayor?" asked Coach LaFleur.

"Oh no this marathon is not over."

Kinny quietly slipped out from underneath the tarp, and crawled through the crowd and back into the visitor's dugout. There she remained quiet, as she recovered from the crash of the Fuller Brake truck into the Gunderson's Grocery float.

"In fact," said the mayor, "the last marathon instruction comes from Deputy Measure!"

Everyone looked around curiously. Teddy was anxious. "He's here ... Where is he?"

Puzzled, Terri joined everyone to look around for Deputy Measure. Then unexpectedly, a police siren bleeped and blarped from the direction of the Main Street Gate. Teddy and everyone else's attention moved from the pitcher's mound to center field where a police car appeared. As it cruised into the Old "B," lights flashed and the siren blurted. It was Deputy Al Measure, delivered back to the marathon at a slow, parade pace.

Chapter 26

The Final Run

Teddy watched with the rest of the crowd as Deputy Measure, with his bandaged arm slung out the passenger window, tried to wave with his good arm. Mayor Tabbshey took to the pitcher's mound and cheered. The coaches and teams moved closer to home plate, as Measure's car stopped. The door opened and he got out with help from the door to steady himself. "My hero and yours," cheered Mayor Tabbshey, "Deputy Al Measure!"

With a shaky step forward, Measure waved. "Thank you."

Nate handed the deputy a piece of paper and he put the information to work. "Dominion Daughters," he ordered, "take the visitor's dugout and Pirates take the home dugout."

The players took their dugout places and Teddy said, "This is good … very good."

"We gonna' do okay?" Tape looked over.

"Sure," Teddy smiled. "You know what I mean, jelly bean?"

When the Pirates heard Teddy provide the 'Jelly Bean' promise, they all popped up and Tape started to dance the '*You Know What I Mean Jelly Bean*' dugout dance. With hips, and knees, and elbows going in all kinds of crazy directions, the Pirates had some fun, as the coaches and town officials looked on wondering if there would ever be a reason to things after Old Luke.

Teddy paused from his Jelly Bean Dance, as he did not want to lose sight of his competition. He saw the Dom Dots seemed to appreciate the kind of seventh inning stretch. Then he saw the Soccer Tommie and Baseball Mommy fans head into the Old 'B' stands. Perhaps a little embarrassed, Teddy saw the town officials and Mayor Tabbshey try the Jelly Bean Dance, too.

"Oh my," Teddy looked across the diamond. He saw Terri step down into the visitor's dugout shaking her head.

"Look its working," exclaimed Teddy, "They are succumbing to some serious *Jelly Bean Mean Trauma*."

Just as Teddy said the words, he saw Kinny pop up to peek around.

Then Teddy watched as Kinny received a hug from Terri. "Kinny!" Teddy heard Terri exclaim.

Teddy paused and smiled, until he saw Kinny limp. It looked like Terri said, "My Kinny!"

Teddy was relieved Kinny had Terri's attention and then looked around to see Munch sprawled and asleep despite all the Jelly Bean dancing. Teddy listened.

"Hey, Munch," Chris snapped. "Get up! It is time for you to show 'em you are a Frisbee dog, too." Munch shifted, snorted, and continued with his seventh inning sort of mid-marathon dognap.

At the pitcher's mound, Mayor Tabbshey swaggered and called for all to hear, "And now it's time to finish the 'Al Measure Founders' Day Frisbee Marathon'! Deputy Measure, will you please announce the marathon's final Frisbee orders."

"Terri and Teddy Fabiano front, and center," instructed Measure.

Teddy winced, and with a quick look to his teammates, he quipped, "Time for *Marathon Accountability Trauma*."

"The Fab 2 goes to second base," directed Measure.

"And let's move Andie and Nobby out into deep center field," pointed the deputy.

Nobby looked across the diamond at Andie, puzzled. "Take the Frisbees with you," Measure clarified.

"Yes sir," Andie replied.

Teddy watched as Andie and Nobby jogged side-by-side into center field after the exchange of high-fives with their teammates at second base. He then looked back to see Deputy Measure cup his free hand to his mouth and shout, "On my count. Nobby and Andie race to second base with their Frisbees. When they reach second base, Terri and Teddy will run from second. Terri will run around first and Teddy will run around third. Then sprint all the way to home plate where the Fab 2 will try to make a Frisbee catch as close to home plate as possible. The closest successful Frisbee catch at home plate wins."

Teddy shuffled his feet as Terri whispered, "The Dominion has you now, Little Brudder."

"Doesn't matter," grinned Teddy. "I am where I am supposed to be, doing what I'm supposed to be doing … when I am supposed to be doing it."

"Doing what," teased Terri.

"You'll see," grinned Teddy, and then he snarled, "Arrr-B-Darrr."

Deputy Measure stepped back from home plate and looked up to take in the wonderful sunny day. He took in a deep breath and felt the warm air in his lungs. Then Measure returned his attention to those around him, and called out for all to hear, "The Frisbee catch first and closest to home plate wins home field advantage here at the Old 'B'!"

Cheers from the heart of the Old 'B' overwhelmed Belleville's latest, most appreciated hero. Measure motioned for Nobby and Andie to get ready for the final stage of the 'Al Measure Founders' Day Frisbee Marathon.' Nobby and Andie set themselves to compete.

Teddy and Terri were set at second base. "The Pirates have you now," Teddy sneered.

"On your marks," Measure liked the tension of free-spirited competition.

"Get set!" The competitors concentrated.

"Have fun, and ... 'Go'!"

From center field, Andie and Nobby raced through the makeshift soccer pitch and on to second base. "Go Nobby go!"

"C'mon Andie," Terri hollered. "Let's get that *Home Pitch Advantage*!"

Chapter 27

Floating Frisbees

Nobby and Andie raced to second. Andie tagged Terri to send her sprinting around third base. Nobby tagged Teddy who chugged to first. The Fab 2 reached their bases at the same time. Just how Teddy caught up, no one was sure. Terri rounded third base cleanly and ran for home plate. Teddy stumbled at first base, then put his head down, and bulled ahead, "Arrr-B-Darrr!" With a quick glance over her left shoulder Terri hollered, "Now Andie, c'mon throw it!"

Andie let go of the Frisbee and watched as it sailed slowly into the air, high over the pitcher's mound and on its way toward home plate.

"Run," Nobby urged. "Teddy run, run, run!"

It was then Teddy called for the throw of the blue Frisbee. "Let it fly, Nobby!"

Teddy felt himself slow between first base and home plate. "Throw it," he urged. "I'll get there!"

Nobby released a smooth throw and looked on as it drifted toward home plate. "It's *Frisbee Trauma Time*," said Nobby, loud enough for Teddy to hear.

"It sure is," growled Teddy as he looked over to see Terri lose track of her distance to home plate. She stumbled. Teddy charged hard to home plate, determined to win the marathon for the Pirates.

Above it all, the red Dominion Frisbee floated gently toward home plate. Teddy saw the blue Pirate Frisbee sail toward home plate and begin to hover. He gasped, desperate to keep his legs underneath him. Despite all effort to close the distance to home plate, Teddy appeared to have no chance. The Fab 2 looked up together, to see the red and blue Frisbees start to dart and dance in the Adam's Mountain breeze. Terri regained her balance, and raced toward home plate. Teddy pumped and churned his legs as the Pirate growled, "Arrr-B-Dang-Darrr!"

In the background, the Old 'B' crowd watched Teddy, and then Terri and then back to Teddy as the Fab 2 sprinted underneath the hovering Frisbees.

Terri neared the plate, and gritted her teeth for an intense finish.

Teddy felt the fire in his gut, determined to finish the very best.

Then Terri stumbled again and Teddy could hear the teams go crazy. He did not look up as the Frisbees fluttered closer to home plate. Suddenly, Teddy realized they had no chance to catch their Frisbees. The timing was all wrong. The Frisbees were floating too high in the air.

The Old 'B' crowd also saw things for what they were and moaned with disappointment. Mayor Tabbshey stared into the many disappointed faces. He had hoped for a strong finish to this Frisbee Marathon.

As the Fab 2 ran their hardest, Teddy heard a cheer. "Come on Terri!"

"Don't settle for anything less than the best--" ordered Coach LaFleur.

"Terri, look out!"

All, including Teddy, looked toward home plate.

Coach LaFleur craned to see the action. Her nails clicked and clicked as she yelled, "Heads up, Teddy!"

The Fab 2 did not hear the warning. It came too late, as they ran hard toward home plate in the greatest effort to compete for the last of any meaningful space on earth. It was all gutsy as the determined players reached home plate at the same time and collided with an incredible force and collision. "Ugh!"

"Oomph!" was all Teddy could say as the breath knocked right out of him.

The devastating impact left everyone to wince and cringe with spines shivering.

Instantly, the wreck was lost in clouds of red dust and soot. Few noticed how the red and blue Frisbees mystically hovered over the colossal collision at home plate. Gracefully, peacefully, as if to wait for the Fab 2 to sort out their business below, the Frisbees patiently soared and circled.

In the home dugout, Chris looked down to call Munch. However, the dog already burst from the dugout and was focused, determined to grab the blue Pirate Frisbee before it hit the ground.

"Munch is *On Mission*," Chris cheered. "Go get that Frisbee!"

With slobber flying, Munch was a big dog missile, galloping along. Locked on target and loaded with a desire to pull down and munch his very first airborne Frisbee.

In the visitor's dugout, Georgia was the first Dom Dot to see Munch bolt. She called out, "Coach ... the Pirates have a secret weapon!"

Desperately Coach Shimpock scanned the Dominion bench to find a counter measure to Munch's undeniable commitment to win. Then Shimpock saw Kinny get up from her corner. In pain, but Kinny had the look of a "Winner."

Coach Shimpock paused.

Andie offered, "Put her in, coach."

Coach nodded. "Kinny you're in. Go to the red Frisbee!"

In a flurry of scrambling black and white fur, Kinny blasted up the dugout stairs and onto the baseball diamond. A fearless spirit and determination overcame her pain as she bolted straight toward the red Frisbee still hovering above home plate.

The Fab 2 tumbled and kicked-up dirt and dust as they wrestled to gain some advantage. Meanwhile, Kinny and Munch raced toward home plate. There was no hesitation in either mascot as Chris cheered Munch, "To the blue ... to the blue!"

Coach LaFleur's nails ticked and clicked furiously, as the Pirates took up the chant, "To the blue ... to the blue ... to the Pirate blue!"

From the batter's box Coach Shimpock yelled, "The red Kinny!"

"Grab the red," cheered Andie. She was sprawled on her belly to see underneath all the red dust billowing around home plate.

The Dom Dots cheered, "Grab the red ... grab the red ... grab the red for the Dots!"

Kinny raced to the cloud of whirling red diamond dust. Then Munch was a split second from the hot catch zone. The Old 'B' spectators gasped as Kinny and Munch both jumped high, and then sailed, disappearing into the roiling red dust in search of their Frisbee targets.

The Old 'B' crowd began to cheer anxious and wild as the flying fur and Frisbee action was furious.

Terri and Teddy rumbled, and then they heard the cheering grow louder. "Hear that?" Terri asked Teddy.

"What's going on?" Teddy was also blind to the efforts of the mascots that now passed over them.

"I don't know," said Terri, "but I thought I heard a 'woof'."

The Frisbees drifted in and out of the massive dust storm created by the home plate tumble and rumble that churned up the clouds of red powder.

"It looks like a little tornado whipping up," said a Pirate fan.

"Yeah," said another fan. "Let's call it 'Little Luke'."

The Old 'B' crowd craned and peered at the suspended Frisbees, as the airborne mascots headed straight into the eye of 'Little Luke.'

"A dang 'Mini-Red Luke," yelled a Dominion fan.

Very curious, Nate approached the red dust tornado. Then he started to call the action play-by-play. "Munch is airborne and zeroed in on the blue Frisbee."

Munch let go with a great, "Woof" heard by all.

Nate then changed his angle, and saw Kinny airborne and already locked onto the red Frisbee. "And Kinny is high in the air, locked on to the red Frisbee!"

Kinny let out a sharp bark, as the Soccer Tommies in the Old 'B' stands went wild with excitement.

"Munch's mouth is open wide and the slobber--" Nate called out. "Oh the slobber...."

Then Kinny flew past. "And there is Kinny. Oh no ... Munch and Kinny are headed straight at one another!"

Teddy lay on his back right in the middle of 'Little Luke.' He watched as Munch strained for his Frisbee, close enough to munch down hard. Now both dogs flew through the air with Frisbees in their mouths.

Teddy listened as Nate called out, "The dogs have their Frisbees. Which one will land closest to home plate?"

From the stands the Old 'B' crowd cheered, "Go Pirates!"

"Get 'em good Dominion!"

Then Nate called out, "Munch's Frisbee has flipped up in his face. He can't see and he's drifted off course!"

Teddy gulped, as from deep inside 'Little Luke' he saw Kinny react and twist in mid-air to avoid an airborne collision. Then Teddy heard, "And it is a great turn-and-twist-away by Kinny!" Now they are certain to avoid a mid-air smash-up!"

The dogs passed through the dust with their coats of hair brushing ever so lightly. Nate was incredulous. "A direct hit is avoided!"

Both mascots fell toward home plate as the Fab 2 scrambled to make way for the Frisbee dog landings.

"And they are coming down for their landings," called Nate.

Both Munch and Kinny made hard, but safe landings in the dirt around home plate.

"Oh, and it's a three point landing for the four legged critters. First the butt, then the nose, and watch how they tumble hard to get as close to home plate as possible!"

With baited breath, the Old 'B' crowd, be they Soccer Tommies, or Baseball Mommies looked for any clue in an effort to decide which canine competitor would emerge from Little Red Luke victorious.

"Man," Teddy could hear Mayor Tabbshey whistle, "I mean what is it gonna' take to decide who gets the Old 'B' home field advantage?"

Chapter 28

Safe At Home

Teddy got up to look along with Nate to determine the outcome. Now the unofficial home plate umpire, Nate tried to make and sell the right call. "Have they got their Frisbees?" a member of the crowd hollered. "Was a frisbee dropped?" asked another.

"Wait," Nate held up his hand. "I see both dogs have their Frisbees!"

Teddy glanced over to the visitor's dugout, where the Dominion Daughters cheered and charged out to go crazy with celebration.

"Kinny," Andie shouted with laughter.

Then Teddy saw his Pirate teammates bolt from their dugout to laugh and holler silly for their celebration. "Munch," cheered Chris. "You *are* a Frisbee dog!"

Teddy watched the events nervously. There needed to be a decision about a winner and quick. He knew the play at the plate needed a call that would sell as a *No-Doubter*. Then Teddy noticed the mayor's look of concern. Nate was holding his pose at the plate, readying to make and sell the biggest call he was ever going to make as a Belleville umpire.

"What is the matter, mayor?" asked Teddy.

"I'm not sure," pondered Tabbshey who turned to listen to the crowd and others.

"You worried about another red mud rumble?" asked Deputy Measure.

"Not really," said the mayor, just as Kinny limped from the dust, Frisbee in mouth.

"More like a red dust fumble.

"And it's…" Nate began to yell his call, but hesitated. He was listening to Mayor Tabbshey.

Can anyone else see what is wrong with this picture?" asked the mayor.

A happy Munch emerged from the dust with his Frisbee dangled from his slobbery muzzle.

"You worried about a tie?" asked Teddy.

Nate stepped into the dust to finish making his call.

"Nothing ever good about that," Measure looked down, as the teams began to rumble in a gleeful kid chaos around home plate.

"Hold on Nate," directed Mayor Tabbshey.

Nate froze. He held his call and the statuesque pose looked painful. Looking over, Nate had a great question knitted into his expression.

"You can't make the call," argued Mayor Tabbshey.

"Mayor you have to argue the call after I make the call," argued Nate.

"Just hold on."

The teams rumbled as Teddy shouted into the fray, "Hey Terri!"

"What?"

"You know what *Coca-Cola* means in Chinese?"

"What?" Terri giggled, as she tossed Nobby to the ground with a floppy hip toss.

"Bite the wax tadpole," blurted Teddy as he grabbed Andie's ankle and pulled.

"No way," Terri laughed.

"True," Teddy grinned as the Fab 2 pondered whether to dive back into the rumble pile that now replaced the pesky fury of 'Little Luke.'

Teddy stood back from the fray and watched as the kids played on. He noticed Nate join Deputy Measure and the mayor looking uneasy. Then he overheard Tabbshey ask, "The Dominion critter is Kinny, right?"

"Yep," answered Nate.

"And Munch the Saint Bernard," continued the mayor, "the Pirate's mascot right?"

"Yes sir," answered Deputy Measure.

"Observe," directed Tabbshey. "The Dominion Dog, Kinny has the blue Pirate Frisbee and that big old Pirate dog has the red Dominion Frisbee."

"Doesn't look good," said Deputy Measure.

"Now how'd that happen?" puzzled Nate.

"Well, aren't dogs sort of color blind?" offered Teddy.

"You thinking some kind of disqualification?" asked Nate.

"No," answered Mayor Tabbshey. "Then the day would be all for nothing."

"But if we let it go?" questioned Deputy Measure.

"Let go of what?" asked Terri.

"Can't pretend to ignore something like this," counseled Nate. "We just can't--"

Teddy listened, but Nate could not complete his thought. Then Teddy watched as Kinny limped toward Coach LaFleur with the blue Pirate Frisbee.

"Well I just don't see how--" Mayor Tabbshey tried to finish Nate's thought, but could not. "Look! The Dominion dog dropped the blue Pirate Frisbee at Coach LaFleur's feet!"

"Well I'll be," grinned Nate. "Kinny returned the blue Frisbee to the Pirates."

"And look there," Mayor Tabbshey pointed again, as Munch dropped the slobbered-up red Dominion Frisbee at Coach Shimpock's feet.

"Never seen anything like it," said Deputy Measure. "Munch returned the red Frisbee to the Dominion."

"Dogs are color blind all right?" Nate investigated Teddy's question further, "So how can they know--"

The Fab 2 listened as the mayor joined in with Nate's field investigation. "Those dogs are setting an example, aren't they," asked the mayor.

"Yeah," said Teddy. "Sure looks like it."

"Like working together," Terri added to the conversation.

"And you know the Dominion and the Pirates actually shared the field to prepare for this big ol' marathon," observed Teddy.

Both Kinny and Munch joined what was left of the playful home plate rumble and tussle.

"And not a single complaint from anyone before the parade," noted Deputy Measure.

"You're right." Mayor Tabbshey looked on, as the Fab 2 arrived at the pitcher's mound.

"So where we going to build the new soccer pitch?" demanded Terri, grinning.

"Looks like this town needs a lot more room for the Soccer Tommies to play," agreed the mayor.

"Yep," agreed Teddy.

"You sure about that?" challenged Deputy Measure, still unsure about the outcome.

"Yep," Teddy laughed. "After all this, I'm pretty sure."

"How are you so 'sure'?" Nate tested.

"Because," Teddy snorted, "the only thing decided by this marathon, was that we were already where we were supposed to be … doing what we were supposed to be doing … when we were supposed to be doing it."

"Yes we were," Tabbshey agreed.

"Sure. The only thing decided," Teddy took in a long breath, "was we proved we all in Belleville can fiercely compete and still get along just super fine."

"So everything is okay?" the mayor asked Terri.

"Oh, we'll be alright," said Terri, "We'll all be good soon as this red dust settles once and for all and we get over this *Unbelievable Old 'B' Trauma*."

Chapter 29

The Counter of Success, Again

The next day, Terri and Teddy cheerfully stumbled through the door of the Belleville Sports Store and saw Nate at the Counter of Success. Nate peeked out from behind stacks of red and blue Frisbees as Deputy Measure leaned against the counter and looked down to see Kinny hobble along behind the high-spirited Fab 2.

"Hey Mr. Nate," Terri greeted. "I hear the marathon is going to happen every year."

"Like the Super Bowl of Frisbee floppiness or something," Teddy grinned. "I can see it now … 'Frisbee Marathon II'."

And years from now we will be watching 'Frisbee marathon XVII'," joked Terri.

"Just think how good the commercials will be by then," Teddy kidded some more.

"Hey, look at the time." Nate laughed and looked at his wrist, but everyone knew there was no watch.

"Yep," agreed Terri. "We gotta' get to practice."

"*We* gotta' get to practice'?" asked Deputy Measure. "What's with the 'We'?"

"Teddy and I have soccer practice now," smiled Terri. "We practice baseball tomorrow."

"Playing two sports?" Measure grinned.

"Yup," said Teddy. "All great athletes do ya know."

"Really," Measure smiled. "And how is that?"

"I'm showing my sister how to be a five-tool ballplayer," Teddy beamed, "with a *Sixth Sense* for winning the games within the big game."

"You have the intangibles covered I see."

"And," Terri clucked, "I'll show Teddy how to be a kick -- um," Terri checked her language, "to be a great goalie and a super net-minder, too!"

"Well in that case," Nate grinned, "I almost forgot about something." Nate pulled an inflated shiny red, white, and blue soccer ball from behind the counter.

"Hey, wow!" exclaimed Terri. "It's beautiful."

"But I," Teddy stammered, "I'm still suffering from *Extreme Cashola Trauma*."

Both Teddy and Terri glanced over at Deputy Measure with remorse. They knew they had the money at one time, but lost it because it was ill-gotten gain.

"I figure," Nate placed the ball on the counter, "you twins have done about as much as anyone for getting Belleville right again after Old Luke. So here, a little something in appreciation for--"

"Besides," interrupted Deputy Measure., "we had to use the money you raised in that Adam's Mountain Highway Radar scheme of yours for something good, didn't we?"

Terri took up the ball with a smile. "Thanks ... wait ... hey it's signed!"

"Signed by whom?" demanded Teddy, as he grabbed for the ball and missed.

"The Olympic soccer team," beamed Terri, "and Mr. Cott, too!"

"Mr. Cott, too?" crowed Teddy. "That is oh so very KEWL!"

"But what do we practice with?" Terri realized the problem with a signed ball.

"Oh, here is another one you can play with," Nate placed a second ball on the counter.

"Thanks Mr. Abelard," the Fab 2 chirped, "Thanks," was the word repeated as they, along with Deputy Measure headed to the door.

Left to mind his store, Nate rearranged the red and blue floppies stacked on the Counter of Success and whistled. In a moment or two, Teddy reappeared at the front door. He had forgotten the unsigned ball and popped his head back in the door, just in time to see Nate grab up a green Frisbee and toss it lightly in the air. Then Teddy heard Nate mumble, "You know, these days it's getting harder to pick the winners."

"Hey there--" said Teddy.

"Shoot ... the champions are finding me so fast, I have a hard time figuring their athletic promise and holding before anything even gets going ... Oh hey there Teddy."

Teddy just smiled, nodded, and decided to come back for the other ball, later.

Later in the week, about halfway up the Adam's Mountain Highway, Teddy and Terri again faced traffic headed down Adams Mountain. They watched as vehicle after vehicle slowed down. The motorists looked through their windows, and laughed at the sign. "I SURVIVED 'THE AL MEASURE FOUNDERS' FRISBEE MARATHON'." Behind the first sign was Teddy.

A hundred yards down the Mountain, the drivers again smiled as they saw Terri's sign. "SLOW DOWN. AVOID THE SKUNKS IF YOU WANT TO HAVE A SWEET SMELLING DAY." Behind the second sign was Terri. Her smile was broad and bright.

Just after the roadside messengers stood Deputy Measure to monitor the community-service that the Fab 2 performed in exchange for their radar disruption caper. Then, unexpectedly Measure looked up the road and saw Tape riding a wheelie, brakeless, witless toward them. Measure stepped out to stop the daredevil lad. "Son … Hold on there. This is not safe!"

"Don't worry Dad," waved Tape, as he rode right on by. "This is my last one!"

"It better be," scolded Measure, not in any mood to chase down his crazy kid.

"I'll follow him," volunteered Teddy. "Make sure he doesn't do anything stupid."

"I think it's too late," suggested Terri, looking back.

"You mean there is stuff 'more stupid than that'?" the deputy cringed.

Teddy watched from his bike as Tape passed beneath the Founders' Day Parade banner over Main Street. It was his finish line. It was where he put down his front wheel and slowed down along Main Street.

Teddy caught up to Tape and pulled alongside as they both came to a stop. Tape looked on as Nate swept outside his store. Then the mayor approached with a wave toward G-McMa before he headed into Murray's Cafe.

"Look," Tape saw Mr. Cott, the elderly Olympian along Main Street.

"Hey Mr. Nate," smiled Tape. "Mayor, how are you doing this fine day?"

Nate smiled, "Hi Tape."

"Hey Mr. Cott," offered Tape.

"You do that crazy wheelie stuff?" grumbled Mr. Cott.

"That was my last one," said Tape.

"Last what?" asked Mayor Tabbshey.

"My last *Adam's Down the Mountain Wheelie*," explained Tape. "I ride down the mountain on my back wheel, most of the time with no hands."

"You're the guy my police department is always complaining about?" asked the mayor.

"Me?" Tape grinned, given the cool notoriety.

"Yeah you," Tabbshey's eyes squinted to serious slits.

"You know that is not some kind of Olympic event," scolded Mr. Cott.

"Not yet," Tape smiled mischievously.

"You ride 'wheelies' all the way down the mountain?" asked Nate incredulously.

"Been doing it since I was eight," Tape nodded. "I perfected going brakeless, witless, down the mountain long before those Fuller Brake folks tried it and screwed it up for everyone."

Nate closed his eyes in silent prayer. "You know, we don't need any more people going brakeless, witless down the mountain."

"You got that right," Tape agreed, chattering over his shoulder.

Nate looked up. "Wait--"

"Gotta' go," hollered Tape. "I'm going to the pound and adopt me a great dog."

"Oh?" said Teddy now interested. "Hey wait!"

Tape held-up and waited as Teddy caught up. "It's a responsibility you know," said Tape.

"Sure is," agreed Nate.

"Good luck!" said the mayor.

"Thanks," Tape waved.

"Going to be a Frisbee dog?" asked Teddy.

"Might be and maybe not."

"And that is okay too," the mayor waved as Tape and Teddy rode off, with thoughts about rescue dogs, and strong practice.

Later that morning, Teddy sat with Terri and visited with G-McMa on her porch. After a couple of minutes, Tape walked through the white picket gate. In his arms was a black, grey, and brown Yorkie that wiggled and squirmed. "Now you just settle down." Tape looked down at the tiny dog. Then he looked up and smiled, "Hi G-McMa."

Teddy smiled as they watched Tape hold out the squirming ball of blinking fur. "Here."

"Who's this?" G-McMa was unsure.

"This is a Yorkie dog," Tape beamed. "I got him from the pound."

"Oh." G-McMa did not have words to say, as the dog's little pink tongue stuck out at her.

"He's for you."

"For me?" asked G-McMa in a hushed tone.

"He'll never be Purdue." Tape was respectful. "But you know you just have to have a good critter."

It was then Teddy felt a lump in his throat along with a change in the air. Warm air swirled in with the cool. "Tornado," Teddy murmured nervously.

Terri looked in all directions. "There was no warning."

Teddy stood to see and listen more intently.

"Does he have a name?" asked G-McMa, not paying attention to the Fab 2's extreme weather alert.

"He's yours to name," said Tape.

Teddy looked over to see Tape and G-McMa unmindful of the threatening weather.

"What do you think?" asked G-McMa.

Then Teddy and Terri saw it at the same time. "Look!" shouted Teddy.

"There's a tornado," shrieked Terri. "There is the rotation!"

"It's some miles off," said Teddy, "But it will get here. We have got to get to a shelter!"

"I can't tell which way it's going," worried Terri.

"Doesn't matter," said Teddy.

"I'm thinking 'Frisbee'," Tape grinned, not having heard a word from either Teddy or Terri.

"Or maybe 'Little Luke'," Teddy suggested and then turned his attention back to the looming tornado.

"Why the name 'Frisbee'?" asked G-McMa, curious as she calmed the fidgety dog.

"We have to get to your storm cellar," yelled Teddy, as he took a step toward G-McMa.

"I guess it was the 'Frisbee' thing that got my mind off Old Luke enough to remember some of the pretty important stuff around here," answered Tape.

"But why?" asked G-McMa.

"I like the name 'Frisbee'," Terri chimed nervous.

Teddy could see the tornado getting bigger and bigger and spoke in a nervous tone, "Sounds good because it will automatically make him a 'Frisbee' dog and--" Teddy glanced up. "Can we get to the storm cellar already?"

"But why," asked G-McMa. "You mean because of that big 'ol tornado rainbow out there?"

"The … what did you say?" asked Tape, confused, "A Tornado Rainbow?" He looked in the direction the Fab 2 and G-McMa all stared.

"How do you like it?" asked G-McMa, with a smile.

"It is a tornado wrapped in a rainbow," muttered Teddy.

"A *Tornado Rainbow*," Terri whispered, in awe.

"Well of course it is," scolded G-McMa lightheartedly. "You know what I mean, Jelly Bean?"

"Hey, that's my line," Teddy fussed.

"Not anymore," said G-McMa. "I think I'll name this little fella' 'T-Bow'."

"For *Tornado Rainbow*," Tape stated the obvious. Everyone laughed a good laugh on the porch and as the tornado rainbow quickly vanished into the bright and sunny sky.

As they all shared the cheerful moment, there was suddenly the yap of a little dog coming from Tape's backpack.

"What is that," asked G-McMa, "That wasn't T-Bow here."

"What?" Tape acted as if he didn't know.

"That was Purdue," said G-McMa, convinced. "Oh my, I believe that was--"

"It is Purdue," Tape agreed as he lowered his squirming backpack to the ground. "When I went to the pound he was in the first kennel. He'd been found and I--"

"You found him," marveled G-McMa. "But what will I do with two dogs?"

Purdue scrambled out of the pack and stopped short, as he saw another dog in G-McMa's lap.

"He looks so sad," remarked Terri.

"I'll help you look after them," volunteered Tape, "We'll build some new dog houses … errr shelters maybe, and--".

"We will help too," chimed Terri.

"Thank you," said G-McMa, as the anxious youths looked on. Then she sighed and went still in her chair. The peace she experienced was obvious to all present as T-Bow licked her cheek, and then jumped down to allow Purdue to hop up to his rightful place on her lap. Purdue licked at her cheeks, but there was no response.

"Call 9-1-1," ordered Terri. "We have to call right now…"

Chapter 30

Mayor Teddy

Years later, Teddy thought how G-McMa had spent a couple more happy years with them before she had she gone on to enjoy the final peace and her tornado rainbow. Then he thought of how Mayor Tabbshey had managed the town's folks to get the most out of his town, while always considering what he could do for the town's mother.

Now retired and destined for the Major League Hall of Fame, Teddy strolled from the Old 'B' toward the mountain end of Main Street Belleville. He knew Mayor Tabbshey had managed him after Old Luke, as well as any World Series manager he had ever known.

"Teddy," an older Chief Measure hollered out the open window of his police car. "Is that you, Theodore Fabiano?"

Teddy turned to Chief Measure and smiled. "Sure is..."

"Well, I'm going to have to take you in for questioning." The chief appeared serious.

"Are you going to arrest me?"

"Well, I'm a Yankee and you turned out to be a Red Sox," grinned Chief Measure. "What do you think?"

"It sure is good to see you Al," grinned Teddy, "C'mon over to the Counter of Success to visit."

"You ever get that *Old Luke Fastball* working?"

"You know I was never a pitcher," Teddy wondered how Chief Measure got that wrong.

"Oh that's right," the chief smiled. "You were always in front of the pitching and behind the plate."

Then Teddy remembered, "Seems to me *you* were a pretty good pitcher."

"That was a few years ago," the chief agreed. "Listen, I'll get the word out you are officially in town."

"Sure," Teddy smiled. "I'd appreciate you doing just that."

The men went silent for a moment, recalling good, strong memories until Chief Measure had to ask, "You gonna' run for mayor?"

"Perhaps," Teddy nodded. "I hear this Belleville team is looking for a good manager."

"You know we still have a pretty good run going," Chief Measure smiled and then paused. "Is that Ferrari you're leaning on yours?"

"What do you think?" teased Teddy, wary of how the red exotic car was out of character along Main Street Belleville.

"The registration is expired," reported the chief. "What do you think we ought to do?"

"I'll register it right here, first thing in the morning."

"Good enough for me." The chief smiled. "And thank you for your cooperation Mayor Teddy."

"Mayor Teddy," repeated Teddy, the new name sounded curious.

"Yep," the chief grinned. "As we all know, every great team needs a great manager. I figure it is your turn around here. That is, provided the brakes on that thing work and I don't have to arrest you by tomorrow afternoon because you are driving brakeless, witless down Adam's Mountain with it."

"No worries there," Teddy assured the chief. Then Teddy got a curious look on his face, "Do I have to run? I mean with good brakes and registration and all shouldn't I be a shoe-in for some kind of appointment or something?"

"You never did like running much," grinned the chief.

"Maybe we can elect a mayor using the Frisbee Marathon or something." Teddy almost believed his suggestion made sense. "You know the scoring would be about the same as any voting."

"And that's not 'running'?" Chief Measure grinned some more. "Sounds like you are ready to cause some trouble around here."

"You know it never seemed like running in the marathon," Teddy pondered. "Back then it really didn't seem like running at all."

"Then why all the complaining?" asked the chief.

"Guess it took me a while to figure out what the mayor was talking about, when he said things like, 'It never seems like work, when you feel like you are making a real difference'."

The men shared the moment. Then Chief Measure asked, "Your sister good?"

"You ought to know," Teddy smiled. "Your son finally got those crazy wheelies out of his system and made a good choice when he married a Soccer Tommy superstar."

The chief smiled as Teddy asked, "You think this town will ever forget about baseball?"

"You know," Chief Measure eyed Teddy carefully, "I seriously doubt you will let that happen around here." The chief paused. "I mean really ... you ought to go over to the Old 'B' and take a good look at all the improvements you have been paying for all these years."

"You know, you're right," Teddy nodded. "But I think I'll go over to the Fabiano Soccer Complex and check that out first."

With that, Teddy tipped his ball cap to the chief, and the police car quietly drove away.

Standing by himself now, Teddy thought about how Old Luke seemed to have worked a strange kind of magic, or maybe a bunch of blessings for all of small town Belleville to live by, if they were going to keep goin' and a growin' in all the right directions.

G. Mitchell Baker practiced law for more than twenty years. Baker enjoys research and writing projects that draw him to publish in the genres of young adult stories, contemporary fiction, science fiction, and, the paranormal. Baker has also been fortunate to compete successfully in sports, to include baseball, soccer, karate, and waterskiing. It is this spirit of competition that you may find and enjoy in his latest work, 'Soccer Tommies Baseball Mommies'. This past year, Baker enjoyed coaching baseball, and developing players for an encouraging varsity experience.

Visit me at my 'Anything But a Tired Barn' (Author Website)
http://www.gmitchellbakerauthor.com/

Find me on Facebook:
 https://www.facebook.com/gmitchell.baker
https://www.facebook.com/GMitchellBakerAuthor?ref_type=bookm ark

Follow me on Twitter:
@G_MitchellBaker

Pin me on Pinterest:
http://www.pinterest.com/1gmbdelta505/

Thank You for spending time with the *Soccer Tommies, Baseball Mommies*. I truly hope you enjoyed this story and will consider posting your book review(s) on Amazon and elsewhere.

Cheers,
GMB

July 2014

31523408R00076

Made in the USA
Charleston, SC
20 July 2014